THE LOVED
AND THE LOVING

RONALD KIRKBRIDE

Unabridged

PAN BOOKS LTD : LONDON

First published 1971 by W. H. Allen & Co Ltd
This edition published 1973 by Pan Books Ltd,
33 Tothill Street, London, SW1.

ISBN 0 330 23634 2

© Ronald Kirkbride 1971

Printed in Great Britain by
Hunt Barnard Printing Ltd, Aylesbury,
Buckinghamshire.

THE LOVED AND THE LOVING

At sixteen Ronald Kirkbride wrote *The Private Life of de Maupassant*, only to be turned down by the local library when he tried to borrow his own book, on the grounds that he wasn't old enough to be reading anything so *risqué*. Several of his earlier books make use of his South Carolina Quaker background – *Quaker Trilogy*, *Winds Blow Gently*, a best-seller translated into several languages, *Spring Is Not Gentle*, and *Only the Unafraid*. Changing his literary as well as his geographical terrain he wrote *Still the Heart Sings*, a book about New Hampshire, *Broken Melody*, set in New Mexico, and *Dark Surrender*, a book about Negro life in the Deep South. But the Old World beckoned, and he reversed the course taken by his Kirkbride ancestors who in 1682 embarked on the *Welcome* from England to Philadelphia, and came to settle in England. Since the war he travelled extensively, writing novels with many different settings. *Tamiko* reflects his knowledge and understanding of the ancient traditions of Japan – his wife is a beautiful Japanese. Five of his later novels, *Tamiko*, *Yuki*, *An Innocent Abroad*, *The King of the Via Veneto*, and *The Short Night* have been translated into many languages and have been or are being filmed. Mr Kirkbride died in March 1973.

CONDITIONS OF SALE

This book shall not, by way of trade or otherwise, be lent, re-sold, hired out or otherwise circulated without the publisher's prior consent in any form of binding or cover other than that in which it is published and without a similar condition including this condition being imposed on the subsequent purchaser. This book is published at a net price and is supplied subject to the Publishers Association Standard Conditions of Sale registered under the Restrictive Trade Practices Act, 1956.

CONTENTS

For

STUART GRIFFIN

Who landed in Japan, September 2nd, 1945, as a US war correspondent with the first American occupation forces, and who later became a Public Relations Officer for General Douglas MacArthur's SCAP (Supreme Commander Allied Powers).

What am I doing here
where my people unleashed
the age of horror,

sowing the plague
that will kill us all?
Can I be loved?

Is it possible
this earth will not scorch
the soles of my feet?

LINDLEY WILLIAMS HUBBELL

Study what thou art
Whereof thou art a part
What thou knowest of this art,
This is really what thou art.
All that is without thee
Also is within.

SOLOMON TRIMOSIN (1598)

PART ONE

1945

In the second week of March, 1945, United States bombers devastated Tokyo and other major Japanese cities with incendiary bombs. At 8.15 on August 6th a Super-fortress flying at 30,000 feet dropped the first atomic bomb on Hiroshima – known as 'The Island of Light'.

News Report

Chapter One

It was Joe's first night in Japan. He would have preferred to be alone, to explore the maze of twisting dark streets by himself, to wander through the raw, burnt-out blocks that was Tokyo and get the feel of this occupied country, but he was a new arrival at the Press Club, replacing Walter Coward of the *Los Angeles Times* who had been killed in a jeep accident in Yokohama, and he was expected to mingle with the correspondents and get acquainted. Earlier in the evening one or two of the fellows had spoken to him, gone out of their way to make him feel welcome – Scott Greenway of *Time-Life*, Dennis Garvan of UP, and Bill Kane of the *New York Times* – but they were older and more experienced men, veterans of Guadalcanal, Bougainville, and Manila, and he felt shy and awkward in their presence, like a cub reporter on his first assignment. Actually it was his first assignment overseas, and as he entered the dim and shabby lounge, blue-grey with cigar smoke, he nervously fingered the brass *War Correspondent* pin on his breast pocket to buoy his courage and to reassure himself that he really was in Shimbun Alley, as the billet had been christened, among the most experienced and hard-bitten newspaper men in the world.

The room was noisy and crowded, not only with the resident correspondents, but with their Japanese companions whom they had recruited from the bars and tea houses in the nearby Yuraku-cho and Shimbashi districts. It was the first time Joe had been in such close contact with the Japanese. On the way from the Tachikawa Air Base he had passed a column of soldiers trudging along the packed road in their tan overcoats and peaked caps and dusty boots, downcast, morose, defeated little men with bad teeth and bow legs. In the fields he had seen old women in straw hats and faded bloomers scratching about

11

in the ground for food, and ragged kids fishing in the filthy canals, but now, looking about the lounge, he was both shocked and fascinated – fascinated by the alien beauty of the girls with their classical moon faces and slanting eyes, so dainty and fragile in their bright kimonos, and shocked because he could not understand how they could even consider coming to the club to fraternize with the Americans, so recently their bitter enemies, who had destroyed their cities, killed their sons, and incinerated their children.

A Jap boy in a white coat and tennis shoes was serving behind the bar. Joe elbowed his way through the jostling crowd and ordered a beer. It was a Nippon brand, and as he stood sipping it he searched the room for a familiar face, but they were all strangers to him. The girls sat at the tables with their partners, giggling, their hands over their mouths or folded demurely in the sleeves of their kimonos, and the fellows at the bar all seemed to know each other and ignored him. He stood and hugged his glass, smiling to himself as if he were quite happy to be alone with his thoughts, hoping no one would notice his discomfort. However, after a time he found he was gulping his beer and his glass was empty, and rather than repeat the ordeal, he reached in his pocket for his wallet.

He drew out a hundred-yen note, and passed it to the bartender.

'Put it away, mate. We only use chits here.'

He turned to face a young correspondent about his own age. He was tall and lanky with a lot of hair everywhere except on his lips and chin. His eyes were blue and lazy, and he spoke in a slow drawl which plainly meant to convey that he was an old-timer in Japan and knew his way around.

'Chits?' Joe stammered. 'Of course. How stupid of me.'

The fellow drew a pink slip from his breast pocket and threw it on to the bar. 'That'll take care of it, boy-san. That's Nip for waiter,' he explained. 'It's the only English the son of a bitch knows. You new here?'

'Joe Barrett – *Los Angeles Times*. Flew in this morning from Guam.'

'Sandy McLean – ARC. I know,' he grinned, 'you PROs

12

think the Red Cross boys are a lot of draft dodgers and misfits, but you're wrong. Our job is propaganda. We're accredited correspondents like everyone else.' He held out his hand. 'Welcome to gook land.'

'Thanks,' Joe said, feeling a sudden flash of guilt because he himself, in a way, was a misfit, had no right, really, to be working as a civilian correspondent. 'I owe you a drink.'

'Forget it. We got to be going. The Lootenant here's got wheels for tonight and a party arranged.' He winked at a short, fat officer in uniform with a chubby, perspiring face who stood by his side swaying on his feet. 'Ain't that right, Porky? Joe – meet Lootenant Crutcher. He's stabled with the Eighth Cavalry in the Imperial Guard Division barracks at Roppongi.' He hesitated, looked Joe over appraisingly, then clapped him on the shoulder. 'You got a date? Why'nt you bug along with us? Porky won't mind, will you, Lootenant? There's plenty of tail for the three of us.'

'Sure, I don't mind, Sandy,' said the lieutenant. 'But we gotta hurry. I got word them guys at Special Forces might be coming over. I know these gals are clean, but I don't figure waiting at the end of the line, not tonight, not after putting away all this Jap-crap.'

While they had been talking, Joe's attention was distracted to a nearby table occupied by a balding middle-aged man and a young Japanese girl whom he had just kissed.

She was laughing and turning her head slowly as he tried to kiss her again.

'What's so funny?'

'The first time I ever be kissed. Very strange,' she said.

'Don't you like it?'

She wrinkled her forehead. 'If we do again I maybe know, *ne*?'

He kissed her several times. Her slim, straight body went limp in his arms. Finally she said seriously, gravely: 'Yes, I like very very much.'

Joe turned back to McLean, a sudden hot restive pain gripping his loins.

'Sorry,' he said, 'I'm afraid I wasn't listening.'

13

'I said for you to join us. Be my guest. You never had a Jap girl?'

'Thanks, McLean, but I'm bushed. I think I'll hit the hay – write some letters . . . '

'Your first night in Japan and you want to write letters? You're nuts! You don't know what you're missing. You got to be initiated. Ain't that right, Lootenant?'

'Sure, Sandy. Anything you say. But let's get going. I got to have the wheels back at the motor pool by midnight.'

'Okay. You coming, Joe?'

'Well . . . ' Joe said, his eyes on the Japanese girl seated at the table.

He climbed into the back seat of the jeep which exploded into motion down a dark alley lined with empty pedicabs, turned right into a broader street, bumpy and potholed with rubble neatly stacked in piles, then swung alongside the moat that surrounded the Imperial Palace. Sandy pointed out the main Occupation buildings across the way: the grey Dai Ichi Buildings, the square Meiji Building, the tall Taiso Building, the squat Yusen, and the Imperial Hotel, all brightly lit, each flying the American flag. A few MPs stood before the entrances, their white-gloved hands behind their backs, their white helmets reflecting the bright lights slanting down from the open windows. They passed a street-car crowded to the brim, and to Joe's amazement, an old 1932 Ford chuffing white smoke from its charcoal-burners bolted on the back. And then, leaving the vicinity of the Palace and the pyramided roof of the Diet Building behind them, they entered an area which had obviously been badly bombed out. Efforts to restore the Japanese-style houses with their little gardens, however, were feverishly going ahead. Already a hasty new façade of scrap timber and sheet-iron huts and shanties had sprung up in the midst of the wide patches of scorched emptiness.

Joe noticed that there were no street signs. People appeared from nowhere – hundreds of them coming and going, dressed in kimonos and bloomers and wearing wooden clogs which clackety-clacked on the parched ground. The men carted crates

14

of sweet potatoes and bags bulging with charcoal; the women carried their children strapped on their backs. Joe could see the tops of their shaved heads bobbing about like flotsam in a wind-tossed sea.

A boy on a bicycle criss-crossed in front of them carrying a bowl of hot noodles above his head on a tray. Porky slammed on his brakes, swearing. 'The little runt! Back on Bougainville I'd have killed him. Funny not being allowed to any more. Just can't get used to it.'

He turned up a steep hill and the sweet sharp smoke of home fires mingled pleasantly with the freshness of early autumn. Somewhere in the distance a temple bell boomed, then died out like a lost chord in the darkness. Perhaps it was the memory of the girl back at the Press Club, and the restive curiosity that had gripped his mind and body at Sandy's invitation, but Joe suddenly felt warm and light-hearted, excited. He was going to like Japan. He had felt that way, he recalled, when he had flown over the northern tip of Hokkido before coming in to land. He had looked down upon the mountainous terrain broken by thin ribbons of dirt roads winding through forests of pine and cedar to scattered toy villages surrounded by patches of green, and had thought: This is a beautiful country. Perhaps they'll let me stay here. There's nothing to go back to. Nothing at all.

The jeep drew up with screeching brakes before a small square wooden house perched on the edge of a slope looking down on rows and rows of similar square houses stretching away to a burned-out waste in the distance. Porky had hardly cut the engine when high-pitched shrieks shattered the silence. In the light filtering through the screen door, Joe could see about twenty girls in pink and blue and red kimonos jammed together behind a fence in front of the house like little lambs in a pen. He caught a glimpse of white teeth capped with gold, a mass of black hair, and then Sandy pushed him through the gate behind Porky, who carried a huge cardboard box in his arms stamped USA ARMY.

'You call this a party?' Joe accused Sandy over his shoulder. 'What is this place?'

'You wait,' McLean chuckled. 'This best Mama-san house in Tokyo. You can do anything with these girls – turn them inside out if you want. If they don't like it Mama-san whips 'em.'

'Why don't they run away?'

'Mama-san owns them. She buys them from the poor farmers. If they do take a powder the cops arrest them and bring them back.'

They took off their shoes and entered a large room covered by straw mats with paper doors leading off to empty, smaller rooms at the back. A selection of girls sat on their ankles around a low red lacquer table listening to 'Body and Soul' on the radio. In their midst squatted a huge Japanese lady with the puffy mouth and fluted lips of a toad. She greeted the lieutenant with a low bow, grazing her chin on the blue-green folds of her kimono stretched tight over her enormous bosom. Then, acknowledging his gift with a sharp animal grunt, she motioned them to sit down.

While Porky tore open the cardboard box and distributed the black-market gifts, Joe and Sandy sat opposite the girls on the cushions provided. Joe was horrified. If this was supposed to be a joke he did not find it very amusing. Only the Mama-san was dressed in a kimono. The other girls were ugly round-faced creatures with rouged cheeks and frizzled hair which stood straight out, cannibal fashion, from their foreheads. They wore imitation-silk blouses and soiled cotton dresses which failed to hide the sagging nylons and high-heeled shoes given them by the GIs in payment for their services. The rice powder on their noses was caked and cracked, the pencil on their eyebrows greasy with perspiration. Joe closed his eyes in disappointment and disgust. It was bad enough that they were prostitutes, but from head to toe they were everything he felt a Japanese girl should not be: crude copies of what they believed Western girls looked like.

When Joe opened his eyes again he saw that another girl had entered the room on her knees carrying a tray filled with tiny porcelain cups. She wore a loose kimono and white *tabi* socks. Her jet-black hair had been cut so short that she resembled one

16

of the children he had seen bobbing about on his mother's back. She could not have been more than fifteen.

She served them cups of hot *sake*, and Joe noticed that her hands, as small and delicate as an infant's, were trembling. She kept her little heart-shaped face turned away and he could not read her eyes, but he could sense the apprehension in them, either because of the presence of the Americans, or because she feared the critical regard and wrath of Mama-san.

The lady raised her cup, croaked: '*Yokoso irashaimase, America-san,*' then got down to business.

Joe was introduced, and because it was his first visit he was offered the most popular and experienced of the girls – Eiko. On Mama-san's instruction she came and knelt beside him, slipping her hand into his. It was pink and moist, as was her face, and with a shudder Joe withdrew his hand, and said: 'If you don't mind, madam, I'll sit this one out. I really just came along for the ride.'

'Now don't be that way,' Porky said, standing over him menacingly. 'You're hurting the little gal's feelings.'

Joe looked at the 'little gal' squatting beside him, her lips smeared with lipstick, her cheeks caked with white powder to hide her age, and turning to McLean he pleaded: 'Go ahead, fellows. Don't mind me. Maybe later, when I've had some more *sake.*'

'You better hurry up,' Porky said impatiently. 'When the troopers arrive you only get ten minutes. You're holding us up.'

'I'll take that chance, Lieutenant,' Joe said, and as he spoke his eyes fell upon the young girl in the kimono who was again serving the wine.

'*Ah, so! Wakattawa!*' Mama-san suddenly interrupted, clapping her hands. 'Barrett-san have eye for Kimi-san! Very smart, *ne*?' She turned to Joe, shaking a fat finger at him. 'How you know Kimi-san come new to my house today? How you know she virgin girl? You like *shojo*, yes?'

'No, no,' Joe said, blushing. 'You're mistaken. She's only a kid . . .'

'Twelve year old. It high time she fuck. She come here to be fucked.' She reached out her arm and grabbed hold of the girl, then pushed her in Joe's direction. 'You take, *ne*? You teach. You very lucky man.'

'You're crazy,' Joe said angrily, jumping to his feet. 'Can't you see – she's crying! She's frightened to death. I'm getting out of here.'

The woman sat back on her cushion and cackled with glee. 'You big man – tall like skyscraper. You make her cry plenty. Good for virgin. Then she not cry any more.'

'I'm leaving,' Joe said to Sandy. 'Don't mind me. I'll find my way back.'

Porky said sarcastically: 'Then you won't be needing Kimi. I got nothing against virgins.' He reached out and pulled her towards him, leaning her backward, one hand plunged into her kimono. She cried out and he turned and smirked at Joe, then dragged her by the arm across the straw mat into the nearest empty room. Joe caught a fleeting glimpse of her kimono being torn from her shoulders, saw her thin, emaciated body with its small, pointed breasts, rounded, yet still taut with the firmness of childhood, pushed to the floor, saw her naked crotch pitifully bare of pubic hair, and then the *shoji* slammed shut, and silence settled on the house.

But only for a moment. From behind the paper wall came a thin, anguished scream, followed by a slap on bare flesh, then muffled belly laughter. Joe strode towards the door, his jaw set, his fists clenched, then stopped in his tracks as a jeep drew up outside, its horn blaring. It was followed by a second and a third. The high-pitched welcoming shrieks of the girls in the front yard drowned out any further sound in the adjoining room, and soon the GIs streamed in, shouting and rough-housing and calling for beer.

In the confusion, Joe slipped out of the door and walked briskly away along the now dark, deserted street in the direction of the Palace.

Chapter Two

The next few weeks were busy ones for Joe. Big stories began to break, and he had to learn to find his way around in a hurry. Tojo tried to commit *hara-kiri*, Tokyo Rose was arrested, the Japanese cyclotron smashed, the Nazi crowd flushed from their plush resorts in Hakone and Karuizawa. General Homma, who had been responsible for the Bataan death march, surrendered and was sent to Manila for trial. Every day there was fresh copy to send over the wire, and when he was not occupied with news reports he went exploring on his own.

He took a train north to Nikko and spent the day wandering around the National Park and the magnificent Toshogu Shrine, untouched by the war, awe-inspiring and peaceful in its mountain retreat surrounded by forests of cryptomeria. He visited the castle town of Sendai in the Miyagi Prefecture, the island of Miyajima in the Inland Sea, and at Beppu spent the night at a small hotel where he shared the communal hot-spring bath with a Japanese wife and her two teenage daughters. He had kept to the far end of the pool, his eyes lowered, and though his skin had glowed with embarrassment at the experience, the family paid him little attention except to bow their heads in greeting.

These were the times when he felt a warm affinity with the island and its people. Standing on the shore of a lake with its wooded points purpling and the shadows deepening into the sinking sun, or peering up at Mount Fuji, its snow-capped cone threaded with pilgrim roads leading to the summit, or walking up a wide path lined with stone lanterns glowing in the night to cleanse his hands in a sacred basin of lustral water, he would be gripped by a feeling, so strong it could almost have been a premonition, that this strange and beautiful land would one day be his home. It was as if it held a secret for him, an escape from his loneliness and the inexplicable lassitude which had gripped him ever since his divorce. This feeling that this was a new beginning was still an unborn sense, yet something fine and pristine, and he shivered in anticipation when he thought of what lay ahead, in the Japanese autumn and winter.

I'd like to stay here and get to know this country, he told himself. I think I can learn from it. I feel something here, but I don't know quite what it is.

And then returning to his billet late at night through the Ginza, crowded with its forlorn kerbside stalls under the bare lights strung from overhead wiring, he would see the ragged children scampering around the slop cans, an old man lying against the wall, holding up his tin cup with haunted eyes, a prostitute standing forlornly outside her dilapidated wooden shack, and he told himself he was mad to even think of wanting to live in this alien land with its hunger, sadness, and poverty. He had had enough of it in his childhood.

He was born in an old mansion on Bunker Hill in Los Angeles, a grand place once, but a near slum when his parents moved from Chicago to California 'where the sun shines and the blue of the sea meets the green of the mountains where oranges grow in your old backyard,' his mother would acclaim bitterly, looking down from one of the honeycombed balconies on to the street below with its wretched assortment of shops, pool halls, picture houses, bars, bargain emporiums and Mexican dance palaces. Joe, up to the age of fifteen, never saw an orange except in the market at five cents a dozen. And in place of the sea, outside his bedroom window hung banners and bedding and billboards advertising bathtubs and toilet fixtures.

To supplement his father's meagre earnings as a violinist at a local restaurant, his mother took in boarders. When Joe was not attending grammar school he roamed the streets on his own, earning a few pennies by helping in the booths in Olvera Street, once a dump-strewn alley, and later a tourist paradise with its maze of ironsmiths, silversmiths, weavers, fortune-tellers, and bookshops. The shy, lonely boy with his wilderness of unruly blond hair became a familiar figure in the street, and as he grew older, was offered part-time working during the holidays by various owners. He sold beeswax candles at La Candelaria,

20

made pottery at La Orizaba. For a whole summer he worked at a *tortilla* factory on North Spring Street making the flat unleavened cakes of Mexican bread. When he was not working, he explored Ferguson Alley, the Chinese quarter, Nigger Alley, one of the toughest strips in the country, and the Filipino colony. It was like entering a new world, and though he was not aware of it at the time, they filled his heart and mind with a sense of mystery and expectation, served as a source of inspiration which later he was to draw upon when, at his father's death in a bar brawl on North Main Street, he was finally released from the shabby prison of his environment and taken by his mother to live in Santa Barbara where she was offered a job as caretaker of a motel high up in the oak-covered cliffs overlooking the sea and the off-shore islands. There, at the age of eighteen, he was to meet and marry Caroline Winter, one of the wealthiest and most beautiful young girls on the Pacific Coast.

On his sightseeing trips around Japan, Joe rarely took advantage of the Allied free entry to the trains or the almost empty coaches provided for the American conquerors, but joined the seething mob of Japanese who came and went in their neverending search for food. Some found it, carrying their gigantic bundles, but others went to bed without it, bone-tired for searching. Night after night they went out and looked. They crowded on the trains, both early and late. They slept on rice straw beside their tiny fires, or huddled on station platforms. They woke and waited for dawn and the first train, their knees drawn to their chest for warmth, and every evening the same windrush of people came back, some with food, some without.

It was interesting and also painful to see them crowd into the coaches in their cheap tight-fitting suits and dresses. They stood or sat shabbily alike, all rather thin and exhausted-looking, but infinitely patient. The motion of the train threw them back and forth, but they always smiled and bowed when they bumped. They wore brown army putties, faded blue trousers, straw sandals, or black rubber sneakers with split toes. The women, as usual, carried their babies strapped to their backs. They

21

either slept or stared, their eyes wide and searching, their small pink mouths blowing irridescent bubbles.

The faces of the men and women were quiet, docile, helpful – ugly, but good. Joe thought they were not the faces of people who started things and made trouble, only of those who were used and driven, who fought when given reason or told they must, but who would not go out just to pick up stones and sticks and guns. These were people who got hurt, who got killed, who lost, but endured the millennia of time. Timeless people.

Only once did he ride in the coach provided for the Allied forces – on a return trip to Kamakura to visit the Zen temples of Kenchoji and Enkakuji. There was a scattering of tourists on the train – wives of the military – and a corporal in the Air Force almost buried beneath huge cases sealed with PX tape. Not wanting to be drawn into conversation with anyone or have his attention distracted, Joe took a seat at the front of the coach where he could look out at the countryside.

As they rattled over the now familiar rails towards Yokohama, Joe sat watching the clusters of wooden shacks pressed, it seemed, almost against the window pane. Now and then he glimpsed small rice fields hacked from the hillsides and planted so that not an inch of soil was wasted. The paddies were watery green, and the rice, suddenly in shadow, waved and flattened from the rush of the train.

After an hour they reached Yokohama and once again Joe was appalled by the destruction – empty burned-out lots, thick with weeds, ruins of houses, the once proud office buildings mere stacks of rubble. Ships in the bay still lay broken up against the sea wall, and others were awash. Only their rigging and the tips of the masts were visible. Once a thriving international metropolis, the city now lay in ruins. There were no young men about, no children, not even a stray dog. Had they eaten them all? he wondered.

And then they rattled along a broad valley between low hills covered with bamboos and conifers. On their left was a wide beach where fishermen, naked except for their white loincloths, were crushing the fruit of seaweed which stretched for miles. It had turned very warm, and it amazed Joe that in Japan one

22

could go from winter weather to spring weather in less than an hour.

In Kamakura he walked down a wide street planted with azaleas and cherry trees to the northern edge of the seaside resort where he passed through the huge gate supported by its wooden pillars and entered the courtyard of the temple, enclosed by towering juniper trees. He was in time to watch the priests ring the great Kenchoji bell in the belfry, then crossed the bridge to the Shariden temple where the bones and the ashes of the Buddha lay enshrined. He wandered about among the lotus ponds with their lovely red and white flowers gleaming in the setting sun, then walked back to the centre of the town lined with its small curio stalls and antique shops pitifully empty of their once precious treasures.

He came to a neighbourhood that was entirely Japanese. He felt the change from Tokyo, and liked it. He liked the paper windows, the silhouettes of people behind them, and all the soft and gentle sounds of the Japanese world in the evening which reminded him somehow of the world of his youth in Los Angeles, Ferguson Alley and the Chinese quarter which he had explored with a sense of mystery and expectation.

He stopped in front of a small fruit and vegetable shop. Two customers were leaving and the owners were bowing as they walked to the front of the store. Everyone was smiling and talking. Joe paused. There was something about the shopkeepers' faces he liked, something in their brown questioning eyes.

Joe smiled and picked up an apple and asked in Japanese how much it cost, glad that he knew the words. The woman and the man broke into smiles, and then two little girls with shiny black fringes ran out from the back and stood close together gazing at him. One giggled, and then both hid their faces in their hands.

'Harro,' Joe called out, the way he knew the kids would pronounce the word.

'Goot-uh-bye.'

'Okay then, goot-uh-bye.'

'Harro, harro.'

23

Out they ran. Then they turned and squatted, each sticking her thumb in her mouth. They showed their thin brown knees and their white underwear, and he watched the merry eyes peep at him over the skirt hem each held up with her fist. Joe waved, and walked on.

Finally he entered a wayside restaurant where he was served clear hot fish soup, raw lobster, fried prawns cooked in soy sauce with onion slivers, chicken stew bubbling hot in a big tureen, an enormous bowl of rice, wedges of pear and apple, and tiny multi-coloured quail eggs. Obviously the meal had been prepared especially for him, a foreigner, and he felt a pang of guilt remembering the thin, emaciated women and children who roamed the streets of Tokyo.

The moon was just rising over the curve of the bay when he started back to the station. The beauty and peace of the little seaside town must have somehow affected him, for so wrapped up was he in his thoughts that he took a wrong turning and, looking up, was astonished to find that he had passed through the gates of the Temple of Daibutsu and was approaching the huge paved courtyard before the ancient shrine.

In the dim moonlight he suddenly sensed that he was not alone. The slim frail figure of a girl in a powder-blue kimono and *getas* was standing on the flagstones at the foot of the Daibutsu, almost dwarfed by the giant statue which looked down at her through the centuries. As he walked slowly towards her, curious as to why she should come here, eager to understand what possible attraction this monstrous idol could have for her – for anyone – he saw her hands, like the petals of a flower, slip from the sleeves of her kimono, heard her clap three times, and bow her head in prayer.

He approached the Daibutsu and stood behind the girl, trying to share her feelings, her devotion, to put himself in her place. A gentle breeze rustled the trees that circled the courtyard like sentinels guarding a secret prize. The half-smiling yet inscrutable face of the Buddha was bathed in shadow, as was the girl's, and though he could not see her clearly, he was aware that her face was just as inscrutable – and bore the same serene smile.

24

Mystery and magic were in the moonlight. The silence weighed heavily upon him, and the shadows seemed filled with the past. It was true, the past was all about him; he could feel it like a breath upon his cheek. The subtle play of light and shade superimposed themselves and intermingled – vanished causes and effects interpenetrated each other like human thought. He shivered.

He waited, watching the girl standing before the Buddha, and the silence became unbearable. The very trees seemed rigid, listening shapes in a frozen frame of his vision. A strange uneasiness crept over him, a combination of acute misery at his inability to rationalise his feelings and the inexpressible longing for something he was aware of but could not grasp. He was conscious of the earth beneath him and the sky above, and his heart seemed to be beating in rhythm to their breathing. Immense time lifted him like a wave under a boat. His mind seemed to spring to life as the cycles came, filling him with strength – and yet the very awareness of this surge of power brought confusion and sudden panic.

He turned and was about to run from the courtyard when his arm brushed the girl's hand. She swung round and faced him, stifling a scream. Her eyes remained open, but for years to come he was to remember that, in that curious moment, he could not tell whether they were slanted or not. They were very black, like the sky at night, stretched wide with terror. Standing before him, a small defensive figure holding itself tightly together in the moonlight, he saw himself reflected in her eyes: a huge, menacing conqueror, towering above her, who had come to mock, rape, and destroy her. And then before he could stammer an explanation, reassure her, she was running across the courtyard into the shadow of the trees, where the hollow echo of her *getas* on the flagstones died out like the fitful breeze.

The corporal said: 'Hi, there! Have a good day?'

They were alone in the coach, and though Joe found it difficult to tear himself away from his thoughts, he replied: 'Yes, thank you.'

'You're a correspondent, I see. Must be interesting work.

25

Takes a lot of brains, eh? Wish I'd stayed longer at school. Maybe I'd be a colonel by now with my own shack and a string of Jap housemaids instead of sitting on my parachute in the goddam barracks. But my old man needed me in the shop.'

Joe looked up and saw a thin wiry young fellow with sharp features and sly, piercing dark eyes. In place of the huge PX cases he was carrying on the way to Kamakura, now he embraced a selection of beautiful Japanese pautownia boxes which gleamed like still water under the naked overhead light.

'You been in Japan long?' the corporal asked.

'A few weeks.'

'You like it here?'

'Very much.'

'You can say that again! We've never had it so good!'

Joe didn't like his tone, but said: 'You're right.'

'I don't mean just with the gook girls. That's easy. I mean with the dough.'

Joe didn't answer. He had grown allergic to the word 'gook'. He turned away and looked out of the window.

The corporal continued: 'It's amazing what you can do with a few chocolate bars and a carton of cigarettes. The fellows at the base throw them away on the gooks. Not me. I don't need to. Don't misunderstand me, I'm not saying I'm a Casanova, just a realist. Any gook girl'll spread her legs if you treat her right – get her away from her family . . . '

Joe noticed that the door at the end of the carriage had no glass in the window. The Japanese people were pressed tightly against the frame. A student in a high-collared uniform and peaked cap was staring at the corporal, who looked up, met his glance, then turned his back and dug Joe in the ribs with his elbow.

'Want to see something? You're not in the forces, so I guess you're okay. What's your name?'

'Joe Barrett.'

'Herb Kaster,' he said, gripping his hand. 'Glad to know you, Joe. Take a gander at this.'

With the expertise of a conjuror, he opened the largest pautownia box. Under a protective layer of rice paper Joe saw a great many kimonos of different colours, all carefully folded. Kaster lifted the one on top, a cloudy deep peach with a delicate and intricately stitched flower pattern, and pointed a jubilant finger at the small embroidered crests on the sleeves. 'Prince Takeda's family,' he said hoarsely. 'Meiji era,' then quickly replaced it.

The second box contained only one Japanese print. Kaster flashed the picture in front of Joe. It was of a young girl dressed in many kimonos covered by a purple robe against a yellow background. The yellow was extraordinary – like a fine sunlight.

'*Utamaro* – Edo period,' he said, and put the print away.

The other boxes contained what were obviously very valuable pieces of pottery and porcelain – one a rare Arita hand-painted bottle which Joe recognized as eighteenth century.

'They're lovely,' he said. 'They must have cost you a fortune.'

'Not a penny,' Kaster grinned. 'Kamakura is full of artists who're starving. They haven't got any money to buy food so I get them what they want in exchange for their possessions. Some of these things have been in the family for generations. It's a little complicated,' he explained, 'because you're not supposed to let the Japs get to the PX stuff – it's black market. But I deal through a pal of mine I met on the Ginza, a stateless Russian. If the police catch me up I'm doing business with a foreigner. That's legal. The Russians, the Chinese, the Koreans – they're all classed as foreigners and they're all in the business.'

The bastard, Joe thought. What happened to Americans when they went abroad? This fellow back home was probably an ordinary nice guy, but here he became a monster, like McLean and Lieutenant Crutcher.

'Then I suppose I'll be seeing those priceless family heirlooms on display in Shimbashi or Okachi-machi tomorrow,' he said, disgustedly. 'Being picked over by some buxom wife from Texas.'

'Are you kidding?' Kaster laughed. 'They go back to my old man's store in the Bronx. We split fifty-fifty. He's smart – knows the market. Maybe he won't sell 'em for years. Then one

27

day you'll see 'em in a gallery on 57th Street. I figure what I got here'll bring ten thousand bucks.' Again he dug Joe in the ribs. 'Not bad for a couple of choc bars, some beer, and a few cotton dresses!'

Joe didn't turn away this time. He looked the corporal straight in the eye, but if the man felt his contempt, he didn't show it, merely sat back basking in the sun of his shabby achievement until they reached Yokohama, where he got off.

Chapter Three

Dennis Garvan of UP was seated in an armchair talking to a girl who was arranging the newspapers on the table when Joe entered the Press Club library intending to do some research. When he saw that he was intruding, he apologized and backed out of the room.

'Barrett, you young idiot! Don't run away. We're not going to bite you.' Garvan motioned to the girl. 'Haven't you two met? Jane, meet Joe — *Los Angeles Times*. Miss Conway's our new librarian.'

Joe crossed the floor and shook hands with her. She was tall and lithe with a red-head's milky skin and her hair was feather cut, fluffy and almost reddish gold. She wore a tweed skirt, smooth over her hips, and a blue turtleneck sweater.

'Glad to meet you, Joe,' she smiled, looking him up and down with slow, painstaking care. 'Sit down. We've just ordered some beer.'

'Jane's the daughter of Major Conway over at Special Forces,' Garvan said. 'She came to us because she's bored with the cushy, fat-cat boys with their gold braids and spinach — right, Jane?'

'Check. I'm an old-fashioned American girl. I like the Saturday-afternoon heroes, boys with crew cuts and sports coats and dinner jackets.'

'Well, we're glad to have you here.' He winked at Joe. 'I guess you can see why.'

'Dennis Garvan! Don't be a hypocrite. You can't see the nose on your face. You're blind – every one of you reporters!'

'Jane's a bit piqued,' Garvan grinned. 'She thinks we prefer the Japs to our clean-cut American girls, which of course is nonsense. Isn't that so?'

'Frankly, I wouldn't know.'

'I'm glad to hear it. Most of the boys out here are just kids and have no idea what they're getting into. They pick up these ugly round-faced Japs with the gold teeth and greasy bobbed hair outside the PX, and then somehow can't break with them. Can't understand it. Well, I suppose I can. They're good bed companions and smart enough to stick together. Once a guy has made a choice another girl never moves in on the pair. But they're nothing more than tarts – ugly ones at that.'

They were interrupted by the boy-san who came timidly into the room carrying a tray with two bottles of beer and glasses. He set the tray on the table, and started out. Garvan yelled: 'Wait up! Are you a good boy-san?'

'I sink so. Yessah.'

'Then bring my friend a beer.'

'Yessah.'

Joe said: 'No, thanks. I have some work to do tonight.'

'Okay, then beat it.'

When the door had closed behind the boy, Garvan said: 'Funny little short-asses. They're the wierdest,' and drew a packet of cigarettes from his pocket.

He was taller than Joe, with massive shoulders and a big head. He had thick black hair and very dark eyebrows and a square jaw with a cleft in the middle. He was obviously a clever man, and though Joe didn't like his manner, he listened to him because he knew he had been around and felt he might learn something.

'Speaking of Japs,' Garvan said, lighting a cigarette, 'how are you making out with them? Love at first sight, I suppose.'

'I wouldn't say that. But I like the country. Interesting people, the Japanese.'

'Ridiculous is my word,' snapped Miss Conway. 'The men look like little china dogs, the women like Cheshire cats. It's an animal world.'

Joe tightened his voice. 'I'd like to understand them better,' he said, ignoring her. 'Why they do so much for us, like changing a flat tyre and taking nothing for the dirt and the trouble. Why they insist on standing and giving you their seats on the trains. We pay for nothing and get everything. They give us everything, not because they've been ordered to, but because they seem to want to. It's enough to spoil a fellow if he's not careful.'

'Why shouldn't they crawl?' the girl said. 'They lost the war.' She poured the beer and went on: 'They're just working us, buying us, flattering us before they ask us for favours. Dad'll vouch for that. They're scared now because they know we beat them, and they respect it. They know nothing about us yet, but they'll learn. Then just watch out, Joe Barrett!'

Joe said thoughtfully: 'I'd like to know what they really think of us – what's behind the backdrop of their tasty food and heated wine and cups of tea and smiles. I'd like to know the Japanese who are always there, but nobody wants to show me. I think I could learn from them . . .'

'You're an idiot!' Garvan snorted, blowing a blast of smoke from his mouth, then battering it away with his hand. 'Take it easy, kid. Curb your youthful enthusiasm. Be detached. Go slow with the olive branch with these people.'

'But the war's over, Dennis.'

'Is it? Give them ten years, fifteen at the most. They'll be at our throats again – if we let them – which we will.'

'One hundred million loyal hearts beating as one!' Miss Conway smiled sweetly. 'So uniform, so obedient! Don't you know what terrible things result from such blind obedience? You should.'

Garvan said. 'I've got my own slogan for one hundred million loyal hearts: Back to the rice fields, one and all. I'm serious,' he said, pounding the table. 'Get the Japs to give up militarism and concentrate on economics. That's our only chance for peace in Asia.' He snuffed out his cigarette, took a swallow of beer. 'We can do it, but we won't. We'll coddle them because we're afraid of Red China. We'll be pals – for a while. Jane's right. They're scared of us now, but they'll learn. We're lazy and careless – they're not. They'll find ways of getting along with us – until they're ready to work us over.' He finished his beer, and abruptly stood up. 'I've been shooting my mouth off. I've got to beat it. I'll leave you with Jane. She'll talk some sense into you. Like don't try to learn too fast. Just take it easy.' He hoisted up his trousers, pointed his finger. 'Getting to know a country too quickly is like staying in it too long. You'll end up by hating it. Mark my word.'

He waved, and was gone.

Jane Conway said: 'Are you busy tonight, Joe?'

'I've got to do some homework. The war crimes trials start tomorrow.'

'Skip it. The car's picking me up in a few minutes. I'm supposed to go to a party at the American Club, but I'm sick to death of stewed colonels. Take me out to dinner.'

'You flatter me,' he said. 'But I wouldn't know where to go.'

'I wouldn't flatter you, as you put it, if I didn't want to go out with you. You're the first nice American I've met in Japan.'

'How can you say that? We've just met.'

'Oh, I don't know. You're young and shy and naïve – about the Japs, I mean. And lonely. Not like these Angus bulls who strut around as if they've won the war single-handed. I'm lonely, too.'

'I don't believe it,' he said, looking her over now with as much care and curiosity as she had first studied him. He thought that her red-gold hair was the most beautiful he had ever seen.

'Well, if you're serious,' he said, 'we can go to the Daiichi Hotel. I hear the food's excellent there.'

'I'm sick of the place,' she said, wrinkling her nose. 'Take me to a Japanese restaurant. You seem to think so highly of the Japs – let's see what they're really like. Maybe they are the Beautiful People you say they are . . . ' She laughed. 'After all, they're supposed to be descendants of the Goddess Amaterasu, which makes them divine.'

'You don't want to do that. It wouldn't be much fun for you if you think like that.'

'How do you know? Convince me. Maybe they have something to offer – they must by the look of the lounge – they're packed in there like sardines.'

'There's Tenichi on the Ginza,' he ventured. 'I've been there once. They serve *tempura* – about twenty varieties of fish and squid dipped in vegetable oil.'

'I'm game,' she said happily, and jumping to her feet, went to the washroom to fetch her coat.

The long black Cadillac belonging to her father was parked at the front when they passed through the door. A slim Japanese in chauffeur's uniform stood patiently waiting in the street, unperturbed, it seemed, by the snowfall, the first of the season, which settled on his peaked cap, cheeks and chin.

'Jiro-san,' Miss Conway said, climbing into the back seat, 'take us to Tenichi on the Ginza.' She reached in her purse and took out some change and handed it to him. 'Then buy yourself some noodles or whatever you like and wait for us.'

'Yis, ma'am,' the boy said, and closed the door.

They slushed through the streets past the Occupation buildings looking vague in the white darkness, and finally reached the Ginza with its forlorn shops dimly lit and its canvas shelters crowded with people huddled to escape the clawing wind. They drew up before a two-storey wooden house with a glass front, and climbed out. Jiro pulled into a nearby alley, and parked.

Miss Conway peered through the glass door of the restaurant, and said: 'No, thank you. This is not what I meant. It's too shi-shi. And there's a colonel in there with his wife. We'll find somewhere else.' She motioned to Jiro to follow them, and taking Joe's arm, they walked through the snow in the direction of Shimbashi, the black Cadillac following behind.

The streets were muddy, lined solidly with bars. Between the dim red doorways were the ink-black mouths of alleys that led back into the darkness smelling of cigarette smoke, whisky, human dung, decayed vegetables, cooking – the ancient odours of sin and misery. As they walked slowly along, from time to time a dark shape would move, thin, cat-like. A ray of light from some distant street lamp knifed through the dark and outlined the plane of a flat, dark face, or glinted brightly on an open eye. Through the windows of the bars they could see men and women in various stages of drunken passion. Pink-cheeked, tousle-headed young American kids lay in the arms of dark-skinned, red-eyed prostitutes. American jazz music beat throbbingly in the night, mingled with giggles, laughter, raucous yells, the incessant buzz of proposition and counter-proposition.

Finally Miss Conway stopped in front of an unpainted door beneath a railway line which bore a dimly lighted sign: OFF LIMITS. She smiled and pushed it open.

In the gloom of the low ceilinged room they were unable at first to distinguish the Japanese *kyuji* who ran to them babbling incoherent English. Joe leaned against the wall waiting for his eyes to become accustomed to the darkness, aware only of a pair of white shirtsleeves gesticulating wildly.

'No American-san! Off-limit! Prease go. *Habba-habba!*'

'Come on,' Joe said, taking Miss Conway by the arm. 'Obviously we're not welcome. Let's get out of here.'

'Are you kidding?' Turning upon the man, she said: 'Now listen to me. What if you came to the States and we wouldn't let you into our bar because you were Japanese. How would you like that?'

He looked at them blankly, babbling: 'Off limit GI. Go home. *Habba-habba.*'

Miss Conway continued: 'I mean if you'd won the war, which you didn't. You know what you'd do? You'd do this.' And she marched over to a table overlooking a small dance floor, and sat down. 'Whisky and water,' she demanded. 'Two. And we'd like something to eat. *Habba-habba* yourself!'

The man hurried away, mumbling, and Joe sat down at the table beside her. Through the cloud of cigarette smoke he could see now that the room was crowded with young Japanese drinking and listening to a record of Nancy Umeki singing 'Tanko Bushi'. Several of them scowled their disapproval, and one or two got to their feet and moved away. An elderly business man with white hair was kissing a young hostess in the aisle. When he saw the Americans he gave a start, disentangled himself, and disappeared behind a curtain at the back. It was from behind this curtain that the waiter returned with two glasses of Suntory whisky, a large bowl of rice, and a plate of fried fish.

'It doesn't look very appetising,' Miss Conway said. 'But we're here on a tour of inspection, so drink up and let's see what they have to offer.'

The 'offering' came after they had eaten the fish and been served three more whiskies. The lights were lowered and the hostesses gathered on the dance floor, barefooted and naked to the waist. It was the first time Joe had seen Japanese girls not wrapped tightly in the folds of their kimonos, and he was impressed by their slim golden bodies and small upturned breasts. For fifteen minutes they danced to a weird Japanese record which sounded like the hammering of drums and the clicking together of wooden blocks, pierced by the periodic wail of an Asiatic flute, and then the record was changed. The girls regrouped and danced again to a slow strumming of a shamisen.

After two more Scotches Miss Conway began to grow impatient. She was also slightly drunk.

'What a dreadful racket,' she complained. 'You like those girls? You think they're attractive?'

'Fascinating,' Joe said, thoroughly enjoying himself.

Miss Conway was not amused.

'They can't even dance! I can do better than that!' And before he could grab her arm and restrain her, she was on her feet and heading for the dance floor.

She pushed the girls aside, and swaying back and forth, tried unsuccesfully to keep to the difficult rhythm. Realizing that she was failing miserably, and aware of the murmurs of disapproval, punctuated by unmistakable guffaws and smothered laughter – determined to hold the attention of her audience at any cost – she peeled off her sweater and then her bra and threw them on to the table.

Immediately the room broke into a high-pitched clamour. 'Ahhhh! *Are miro! Nantoiu zamada!* Ahhhh!' Chairs grated on the floor as they were pushed back by the astonished occupants who pressed forward in an effort to view that rare and expensive object – the naked torso of a Western woman – seldom, if ever, seen before by young or old.

As Miss Conway continued to writhe and squirm about the floor, the girls fled, protesting, behind the curtain. Finally, realizing that her performance was having the exact adverse effect upon her audience as was her intention, in a sudden sobering moment of confusion and shame, she fell to the floor in a flood of tears. Joe hurried to her rescue, and with the help of the manager, who had recovered her belongings, they were escorted to the door, which slammed shut behind them.

Chapter Four

They drove in silence to the major's house high up on a hill-top in Azabu. The shock of the cold night after the warmth of the bar appeared to have sobered Miss Conway, who let it be known by her manner if not her words that she regretted her unseemly behaviour, and wished to atone for it.

'Please come in for a nightcap, Joe,' she said when they drew up outside the low, semi-Western style house overlooking the city.

'Don't you think you've had enough?' he said grimly. 'And what will your father say?'

'I have my own entrance – my own wing of the house. Daddy never intrudes on me and I don't intrude on him. We have an understanding.'

'It's very late,' he said, uncertainly.

'Please. I want to apologize. I promise you won't regret it.'

She took his hand and pulled him out of the car.

'I'll call you if I need you, Jiro,' she said, and led Joe into the house.

She switched on the lights in the hall and he followed her into a wide sitting-room with polished hardwood floors and hideous blue velveteen sofas and chairs, obviously the pride of the Japanese owner before he had been evicted and his house requisitioned.

She crossed to the bar and poured two Scotches, but she had hardly touched hers when she excused herself and disappeared into the bedroom. Joe paced the floor, wondering with a twinge of excitement if his suspicions were correct, wondering whether he should wait and find out, or slip away into the night. He decided to stay and was rewarded by her plaintive voice calling to him through the door. He entered the bedroom and found her lying naked on top of the blanket, her bright tresses spread out like a halo on the pillow, two tall candles alight by her side. Her hands that lay along her legs were white, her stomach golden, her breasts the colour of cream roses. She lay without shame, like a pleasure garden stretched out before him, and crossing to the bed, he smiled his approval, then threw off his clothes and lay down beside her.

'Oh, Joe!' she whispered. 'Joe! Joe! So long! It's been so long! You don't know!'

And then the long taut length of her body was against his body, the hard nipples of her breasts against his breast, her mouth a devouring flower, her tongue lashing his tongue fiercely, unmercifully, as she pleaded: 'Promise me, Joe! Promise me you won't make love to a Jap girl. Promise me! Promise me!'

Later, while she slept, he lay in the darkness listening to her breathing, trying to explain his disappointment. She had been eager, passionate, generous in her love-making, an expert, like a woman who had learned well from men what pleased them, and yet once again he found himself left with a feeling of emptiness and futility, a hope turned dull and irritable.

He felt he understood her, even after such a short acquaintance. Like so many girls from the States who had found themselves deserted by their boy friends swallowed up by the draft, Jane Conway had come to Tokyo with her father hoping to find a suitable companion overseas. Here there were plenty of young men, but what she hadn't anticipated was that the Japanese girls had taken them all.

36

She had been shocked, unable to believe that these girls, so many of them ugly and penniless, from the rice fields and from the bombed-out ruins of Osaka and Kobe, could possibly possess any quality that could attract a mature American male. She hadn't believed it, and she wouldn't believe it now, for to do so would be to admit to herself that she was being spurned.

Her vanity and pride had been hurt, and she was resentful. This was why she had taken him to the club in Shimbashi to mix with the prostitutes and pimps, closing her eyes to the fact that the Japanese were human beings. By going out of her way to humiliate them, she took her revenge.

He felt sorry for her in a way – as he had felt sorry for Caroline . . .

They had met at the Santa Barbara Public Library one summer day where he spent the mornings at a desk by the window writing short stories and articles which he mailed, unsuccessfully, to magazine editors all over the country. He was writing, lost in thought, when he glanced up and found a young girl with blonde hair and blue eyes looking over his shoulder.

'You're a writer!' she gasped. 'How simply scrumptious! I've always wanted to meet an author. Are you famous!' There was a breathless catch of enthusiasm in her voice. 'I'm sure you are! What's your name?'

He told her, then informed her impatiently that he had been writing stories and verse for two years with only one acceptance – a poem accepted recently by the local paper.

'Of course! "Sunrise", by Joseph Barrett! I knew you were famous! Do you live in Santa Barbara, Mr Barrett?'

'Yes, in Montecito.'

'That's funny. I don't remember seeing you at the Beach Club or the Casino. I suppose being a famous author you spurn places like that. Are you a Communist?'

'Good Lord, no.'

'That's a relief. Daddy has a bug about Communists. We own the Winter tract – that's my name – Caroline Winter – out

37

at Sandyland, and he's scared to death the Communists will take it away from him. Like Franklin D. Daddy says he's a Communist.'

'He's crazy,' Joe laughed.

'No, he's not. He's a poppet. You'll like him.' And then abruptly: 'I'm giving a beach party tomorrow night. Won't you come? Oh, please!'

He pushed back his chair, looked up at her bright blue eyes, at her nose with its gay, challenging tilt, her small, pointed gleaming white teeth, at her red lips which matched the red polish on her nails, and said: 'That's very kind of you. I'd love to come.'

They were married at the little church overlooking the sea one month later. He never did know quite how it came about, except that he had been pressured into it, not only by Caroline but by her parents. He had protested, explaining that he could not possibly support her in the manner to which she was accustomed on his salary as a night clerk at the motel, but Mr Winter, a gentle man with the startled features of a small brown quail, explained, in turn, that money was worth only the pleasure it could give, and that Caroline was exceedingly well off in her own right, while Mrs Winter, a tall aristocratic woman with long tapering fingers crusted with jewels, let it be known that she would welcome a writer in the family even though he should never find a publisher for his works. The mere fact that he *was* a writer and a poet would lend an aristocratic aura to the marriage, adding, in all seriousness, that he had Byron's forehead.

He should have realized at the outset what he was getting into, but he was blinded by Caroline's beauty, her youthful exuberance, her generosity. Where he was concerned, she was certainly a 'catch'. While he had been to grammar school in the slums of Los Angeles, she had graduated from the fashionable Santa Barbara Girls' School. She was accomplished in that she played the piano beautifully, liked to decorate the interior of her friends' homes, and dabbled in water-colours.

They went to Palm Springs for their honeymoon, which Caroline found rather boring, and returned after one week to a six-bedroomed house on the Riviera, a gift from her father. Overnight Caroline returned to the life to which she was accustomed, a life he soon found to be completely alien, even frightening.

At first he was delighted and grateful to have his own study where he could work uninterrupted, wishing to prove not only to Caroline, but to himself, that he could make a success out of his writing. It did not take him long, however, to realize that she hotly resented the hours he spent shut up by himself. At the numerous parties they gave at home, and at the Beach Club in front of her friends, she would kiss and caress him and boast of his work, calling him a genius, but the moment they were alone she became bitter and angry, or simply ignored his work completely, showing no interest whatever.

His main objection and point of fire was these seemingly endless parties. A great deal of it, no doubt, was personal. He disliked most of the people present, and knew they secretly disliked him. He was not of their world. He had nothing in common with them, or they with him. The only person he did see occasionally was Lionel Backler, a tall, angular, shabby young man with a mass of tangled hair whom he had met at the library before his marriage. He came to the house once or twice, his arms filled with weighty books on Socialism by the Webbs and Bernard Shaw, and his rantings horrified Caroline, who asked him not to return, a request with which he willingly complied.

She would drag Joe out of the library in the middle of his work to join her friends on the beach, where they lay about in bathing suits drinking warm whisky at eleven o'clock in the morning. The sand was covered with cigarette ends and smelled of spilled, sun-scorched alcohol. Or in the evenings, after hours of drunken small talk, an amorous couple would sometimes slip upstairs and return looking red and self-conscious. Joe would go up and find his bed mussed and Caroline's douche bag hanging in the toilet. He would come down flushed with anger. The entire house, when the guests had left, was utterly ruined for him.

What really disturbed him was that Caroline's life seemed

dependent on what other people thought of her. It was for them she bought such expensive clothes; for them she laughed so gaily and light-heartedly; for them she played the piano, went to a concert. Never because she liked a thing herself or found a personal need for it. He felt that without these people, without their presence or influence, there would be no pleasure for her in living, no purpose. She would be lost.

With a growing sense of foreboding, he realized that she derived more satisfaction from these people's glances and compliments than from the love he gave her when they were alone. And he began to grow watchful and afraid.

Soon it became obvious to him that there was a connexion between this need of hers for admiration and their life together as man and wife. Their sex life had never been successful. He thought, in moments of frustration and despair, that if her friends had been allowed into their bedroom, had been witnesses to their love-making, she might have come alive as she did at the parties. Alone, it was all mechanical, hurried, unimportant, a ritual that had to be performed if she were to act the part of the happy young bride she wished to appear to the outside world.

He even suspected, incongruously, that she was having affairs, because the only time she showed real passion for him was after a night out on her own. She would then clasp him in her arms, tingling with some hidden joy, as if by making love to others she could bring herself to accept his caresses. But he never questioned her, afraid that if the truth were brought into the open, their marriage would be at an end.

One evening he came home to find Caroline sitting at the table in the living-room with a girl friend and two strange men. The girl was half clothed, Caroline completely naked. As he approached the table he heard her exclaim: 'Here comes the bad news! Now for a lecture!'

He took off his coat and threw it over her.

'All right,' he said. 'Explain. Out with it!'

Caroline put on her sweetest expression.

'Don't get excited, my pet. We've just invented a new game. Strip bridge!' And looking at him with a pathetic little smile which made his heart leap for love of her: 'It's easy to see who's losing, isn't it?'

His presence in the room broke up the party, as it usually did. He felt the scorn of the others, but took no notice of them. Caroline went into the powder room, trailing her clothes behind her. 'Why do you always have to spoil everything?' she said bitterly. 'It was only in fun.'

He didn't answer her, and she went through the door, slamming it behind her.

The marriage did come to an end abruptly one night when they returned from a particularly unpleasant party on the sand-dunes. As he lay beside her in bed, close, but not touching her, he said: 'There's something awfully cheap about those people. I just don't like them, Caroline.'

'Oh, they're all right once you get to know them,' she said sleepily.

'Who wants to know people like that?' he protested. 'Damn it all, why should we waste time on them?'

She turned to him furiously.

'I wish you wouldn't speak about my friends like that! I don't say nasty things about yours, do I?'

'You know perfectly well I have none,' he answered.

'Well, it's certainly not my fault if you're unpopular, and you seem to make use of them. I don't see you missing any of their parties.'

'You know I go simply because you want to go,' he said. 'I don't care for all these drunks and their two-toned convertible minds!'

She sprang out of bed and began pulling her clothing from the wardrobe.

'I've had about all I'm going to stand of this,' she snapped through tight lips. 'You live in my house, spend my money, and insult me.' Suddenly she stopped, and he saw her eyes were full of hatred. 'No, I won't go. Why should I? This is my house. You can bloody well go!'

He did.

Mr Winter coughed, and said sadly: 'I'm not saying it's all

41

your fault, my boy. Of course I've never approved of these people – these bohemians – you entertained at the house. I must say it never occurred to me when Caroline . . .'

'Bohemians?'

'Proletarians, I believe they're called. This friend of yours, Lionel Backler. I've been looking into his credentials. He's a member of the Communist Party – but of course you must know that. I think it was rather indiscreet of you – to put it mildly – to introduce him to my daughter – to involve her . . .'

'Involve her? How?'

Mr Winter sighed.

'I think the best arrangement would be if you left town for a while. I understand from Caroline you have been turned down by your draft board – you are classified 4F.'

'Unfortunately, yes. I'm slightly deaf in one ear.'

'A pity. Not that I would wish any young man to have to enter the Army under the present difficult conditions. But that is neither here nor there. As I was saying, it might be best for you and Caroline if you didn't see one another. A few months' separation, then a quiet divorce. In the meantime I would like to help you if I can. I have business connexions in New York and San Francisco, but of course you wouldn't approve. You prefer the arts. If you have any suggestions . . .'

'I have. I'd like a job with a newspaper – any newspaper that will send me overseas. Can you arrange it?'

'Possibly. Possibly.' Suddenly he beamed. 'A good idea, in fact! I'll see what can be done this very day.'

Chapter Five

Joe sat beside Scott Greenway of *Time-Life* in the improvised courtroom in the Japanese Military College, Ichigaya. Although an older man, Joe had become friendly with Scott. He was tall with a big, relaxed face and deep-set eyes that crinkled with a faraway look in them. His shaggy hair was grey at the temples. Though it was well known at the Press Club that he had saved more than one life during his stint with the magazine – he won the only Silver Cross given to a newsman in the Pacific theatre – his manner was so steady and composed that he gave the impression he had seen very little action. Everything about him was honest, patient, gentle. He seemed sometimes weary, and yet there was about him a funny sense of youth, almost of quest.

'*Attention!*'

Five officers entered slowly from the left and settled themselves behind the high front desks. One was a full colonel. 'Court will permit the taking of photographs,' he snapped.

Joe stood up and shot the court, the crowd, the accused, and the trial counsel, while other American cameramen ran, ducked, and made their shots before the Japanese were given their turn.

'This must be an old classroom,' Joe whispered.

'Have a hunch it will be for the Jappies,' Scott said. 'They'll learn one simple lesson. We won the war.'

'Yes, but they'll get a fairer deal than a lot of them gave our fellows.'

'Why, sure,' Scott grinned, 'the utmost in impartiality.'

So far all Joe had seen of the accused was the bushy back of his head. A Japanese was photographing him full face, one hand holding aloft a small metal tray. *Whoof!* There was a sudden explosion and blue smoke swirled up toward the ceiling.

'Oh, oh!' said Scott, 'the old magnesium flash. Court's not going to stand for that.'

The President of the Court beckoned an MP. 'Remove that man,' he ordered. The defence counsel jumped up. 'You're out of order,' he was told. 'Resume your seat until the trial commences.'

Scott gave Joe a sidelong glance. 'Tell me more about your fair, impartial court. Poor bastard, the only equipment he had, probably.'

The court came to order and the accused rose. He was a slim fellow in blue denim work-clothes. The white letter 'P' was stencilled on his trouser leg, his left buttock, his shirt in two places, and across his shoulders. He wore cheap rim glasses, with the right bow missing and replaced by a loop of twine. His thin, sallow face was devoid of emotion.

His name was Morimoto. He shouted his answers to questions put to him and stood at rigid attention throughout, now and then turning to bow stiffly towards the court.

'Instruct the accused to lower his voice. This isn't a Jap drill field!' said the President. 'Trial counsel may continue.'

The accused bowed once more, but the only sound was the tap-tapping of the court stenographer on a small machine that rested on his knees.

So this, Joe muttered, was Tatsuo Morimoto, alias 'Four Eyes', a former sergeant and chief guard of Camp Ofuna, alleged sadist, alleged murderer of five American prisoners-of-war whose faces he had smothered in liquid manure.

When the evidence, sketchy, hearsay, and circumstantial, was finally completed, the members of the court filed out and a restive rustle passed over the crowd, like the noises in church. Joe, glancing up from his notebook, looked round the room, then suddenly sat straight in his chair.

Among the spectators seated at the opposite end of the room was a Japanese girl in a blue kimono, her luminous black hair falling about her shoulders, her eyes staring blankly out before her. He recognized her at once – who could ever forget that inscrutable face as she stood devoutly before the Daibutsu in Kamakura, or her dark eyes stretched wide with terror, though they were not filled with terror now, only with dispassion.

Sitting beside her was an elderly couple, a quiet, pretty lady in a kimono, and a man with a distinguished appearance dressed in an elegant dark kimono stamped with the family crest. His long pale face was ascetic, yet lighted by swift, vivid glances as he studied the crowd around him. In spite of his beard, which shone with threads of silver, Joe was struck by a resemblance to the accused, and turning to Scott, he asked:

'That Japanese couple with the girl seated under the light. Do you know who they are? The old man looks like the accused.'

44

Scott studied them for a moment in silence.

'You've got a good eye,' he said. 'That's Morimoto's mother and father. I don't know who the girl is. Probably some distant relation.'

'I've seen the girl before – in Kamakura.'

'Then she's probably not related. The Morimotos live in Kyoto. He's the Director of the National Museum – a very distinguished old man. This trial must come as a great shock. If his son is convicted it will mean the end of Morimoto's career.'

Joe was about to question him further when the members of the court filed in. They had been out just fifteen minutes.

'*Attention!*'

The accused rose and faced the high desk that dwarfed him, while the President of the Court read and reviewed the charges and specifications. Then he paused, and his eyes lifted.

'We find the accused, Tatsuo Morimoto, guilty on all charges.'

Something walloped Joe over the heart. Instinctively his glance went to the old couple, whose expressionless faces were chalk white, and then to the girl whose eyes seemed to stare blankly into his. If she recognized him, she gave no sign, and soon turned her head away.

The President cleared his throat.

'Tatsuo Morimoto, you have been found guilty as charged. Do you have anything to say before the court passes sentence upon you?'

There was no reply.

'Tatsuo Morimoto, by a secret ballot, two-thirds or more members of this honourable court concurring, you are hereby condemned to suffer death by hanging. You will now be re-manded to a place of confinement, there to await . . . '

Scott said abruptly: 'Okay, son, let's get the hell out of here.'

At the door Joe saw the girl and the couple again. There were tears on the old lady's cheeks as she followed in the wake of her husband, her small clogged feet shuffling over the wooden floor. The girl, who had broken away from the pair, looked up, and in her startled expression he was sure she recognized him. He could not read her eyes, but her glance was momentarily thoughtful, even a little curious, as if she remembered him but could not place him; and then it became suddenly frigid, and turning her back, she ran into the street and disappeared in the crowd.

He did not know why she remained in his thoughts like a figment in a dream, a person he had never met, yet knew he would meet one day, and when he did, would recognize. On a more practical level, he felt that this girl, as unapproachable as she appeared to be, could perhaps serve as the instrument through which he could break down the barriers between the Japanese people and himself once he had penetrated her hostility and got to know her. It was because she was so unapproachable that he felt that she was the one person who could introduce him to the Japan no one seemed to want to show him, a Japan he could see, but could not understand. She was obviously of good breeding, far removed from the girls who frequented the Press Club or fraternized so freely with the military.

It was with this thought in mind that he went to the Police Station to try to discover her name and address. The police were most kind, treating him with smiling respect, and though they could not be certain of their facts based on the scraps of information he gave them, they felt she might be Hanako Morimoto, the couple's daughter-in-law, the widow of Shiro Morimoto, Tatsuo's older brother. She had apparently left the parental home in Kyoto and was now living in Kamakura.

On Sunday he took a train to the seaside resort, having no plan in mind except to find the girl, at the same time dreading the moment if he should find her, not knowing how he would be received, if at all, or even if she could speak English.

It was a clear, cool afternoon when he entered the town and approached the police kiosk. As there were no street names or house numbers, he would have to act as his own detective. The policeman vaguely recalled the name, pointed to a group of small wooden houses on top of the hill overlooking the village, and waved him on.

He walked up the steep slope until he reached the row of tip-top houses divided by a narrow dirt path, then paused to

46

catch his breath. He swung round and faced a magnificent panorama of the Izu peninsula and the mountains of Hakone. Far in the background, splashed with the fire of the afternoon sun, rose the snow-capped cone of Fuji, and below, like a sleeping monster in the placid sea, the island of Enoshima. And to the east, Misaki and the bay of Yokohama bathed in mist, and further out on the horizon, the smoking volcano of Vries Island.

He had never witnessed a more beautiful scene, and he told himself that, in spite of the girl's apparent coldness, she could not live in such a place without, deep down, being a part of it. The setting and the girl must surely be synonymous.

After approaching several of the houses and displaying the card the police had given him with Hanako's name printed on it in Japanese characters, he found her.

She opened the door and gave a gasp when she saw him. They stood for a moment looking dumbly at each other, he in confusion, she in embarrassment because she was bare-footed and wearing long silk bloomers.

'Hello, Hanako-san,' he stammered. 'May I come in?'

She collected herself with difficulty.

'Who are you? Why do you follow me here?'

Her English was fluent, but stilted, as if it were a skill rather than a practice. There was something of tightrope walking in her speech. He smiled at her.

'I didn't follow you. I saw you at the trial and just wanted to come and tell you how sorry I am – about the whole business.'

For a moment she seemed to weaken, then turned upon him almost savagely.

'You are in America forces? You police MP?'

'No, I'm a newspaper reporter. My name is Joe Barrett. I first saw you in the temple courtyard, and I'm afraid I frightened you. I want to apologize.' He smiled again. 'I've come all the way from Tokyo. Perhaps I could have a cup of tea.'

She stood in the doorway, her eyes bright, her cheeks aflame because he had intruded upon her privacy without being invited and had found her in disarray, unprepared for the traditional cup of tea and cakes which he requested and had every right to expect after his journey.

'Please,' he said. 'I'll only stay a few minutes.'

She led him through the door into the corridor, where he took off his shoes, and then into a small four-mat room sparsely furnished. She motioned to him to sit on a cushion on the *tatami*, which he did, his back to the *tokonoma* adorned with a scroll of Mount Fuji and a single spray of evergreen.

'Please excuse,' she said, and disappeared behind a screen in one corner.

He thought she was preparing tea and, settling back, looked about him.

The room contained a small dresser, an *hibachi* aglow with charcoal upon which rested an iron kettle, and a small lacquer table – that was all. On top of the dresser Hanako's few possessions looked down at him as if from a great distance: her brush and comb, a brown satin doll with yellow hair, a cardboard piggy-bank painted blue, a porcelain brooch, a china deer from Nara, a photograph of a small child in a wooden frame. To Joe they appeared fragile and forlorn – one sweep of his arm would have broken them all. It seemed impossible that only these little things belonged to this beautiful girl with her haughty, disciplined body.

She slipped from behind the curtain, and he was surprised to find that she had changed into a pale green blouse, skirt and stockings. She came back smoothing down her hair, lank to her shoulders. He noticed for the first time that she did not use lipstick and that her mouth, while full and round, still had the petal lips of a child. Her skin was neither white nor yellow nor tan, but a little of each, like golden honey.

She crossed to the *fusuma*, slid it open, and returned with a teapot and two porcelain cups. She put the dark green tea leaves into the pot and poured the hot water over them, then sat down upon her heels beside him. Her movements were so graceful – the small act with her hands and how she moved her fingers – that his heart quickened.

When she had placed the cups on the wooden saucers and

passed him a selection of Mikasa cakes made out of bean paste wrapped in thin pancakes, she said:

'You did not come here to say sorry. Why you come?'

'But it's true.'

'You are not sorry that my honourable husband's brother Tatsuo-san will be executed. If he did these terrible things it is only right he should suffer for it. Why you come?'

'I've told you, Hanako-san.'

'It is only excuse.'

'All right,' he grinned. 'If you must know, I came because I wanted to meet you – is that so extraordinary?'

'*Hi*. Many Japanese girls in Tokyo. Why you come here? I married woman.'

'But your husband's dead.'

'It makes no difference.'

'It must, Hanako-san. Listen to me. Try and understand. I've come to love Japan, but I don't really know much about it. I'm not a soldier with officer status and PX privileges. I'm just an ordinary guy who would like a companion to show me around. Is that such a terrible thing? Couldn't you show me Japan – couldn't we go places together, Kyushu, Shikoku, Kyoto . . . '

'No!' She glared at him, and suddenly he remembered Jane Conway's words: 'The women are like little cats.' Hanako's eyes were like cats' eyes at that moment, wide and slanting. She looked as if she were ready to spit. 'You are a mad American, I think!'

'I'm sorry you feel that way,' he said, and took a bite of cake.

'You think I go out with American? What you think my friends say! American kill my husband, my father, my mother! They destroy Japan! I tell you what they say. They call me filth, scum! No, I not go out with American – ever!'

He waited for her to calm down, then asked:

'Tell me, Hanako-san, how is it that you speak such good English?'

'I went to Christian school when I was small girl. Very stupid thing, but my father's wish.'

'Then you must have met many foreigners – your teachers

must have been Americans or British. You must have realized we're not all beasts and murderers.'

She was silent, sipping her tea.

'Will you have lunch with me tomorrow?'

'No!'

'Where do you work?' he asked.

'Tokyo.'

'At the PX?'

'Never! At Meijiya on the Ginza,' she said, then clapped her hands over her mouth.

Joe grinned. 'I'll pick you up at twelve o'clock. We'll have lunch together at some small out-of-the-way place . . . '

'No, please! I lose my job. You tall American – everybody see and call me filth.'

'I'll pick you up at twelve,' he persisted, and climbed off the cushion. 'Thanks, Hanako-san. I've enjoyed myself. The tea was lovely.'

She was near to tears. All her hostility and discourtesy seemed to melt away, and in its place he sensed, behind her mask of enmity, the lost, bewildered, frightened, wounded person she really was.

'Please,' she pleaded. 'You must not come to store where I work. I meet you front of Shimbashi Station at twelve-thirty.'

'Okay, it's a deal,' Joe said.

Chapter Six

She was waiting for him at the station entrance when he arrived. She was wearing a tweed coat and flat-heeled shoes, her head wrapped in a blue scarf. She barely looked up when he greeted her, and when he offered her his arm she refused it, walking silently by his side as he led her across the muddy street to the nearest Japanese restaurant. He chose a table at the back of the room and attempted to help her off with her coat. She retreated,

50

and with bowed head took off his coat and hung it on a hook on the wall. Then she removed her own and sat down opposite him, her eyes lowered, a picture of servility and resignation.

'Hanako-san – cheer up. This is supposed to be a happy occasion. What would you like to order? The *sashimi*, *tempura*, and *sukiyaki* look good. And a bottle of *sake*?'

'*Sushi* and tea, please,' she said.

He sighed and ordered the same. He felt suddenly discouraged and disappointed. Their date was obviously going to be as short and as uninspiring as the meal.

When the rice balls and tea arrived, looking cold and inadequate, he said in desperation: 'Perhaps we've made a bad choice. Would you like to go somewhere else? To the American Club or the Daiichi Hotel?'

'Very becoming here.'

'You mean nice.'

'So sorry. Hanako speak very bad English. Why you want to take her to restaurant can't imagine.'

'Because I like you. Because I want to get to know you. Can't you understand that?'

'Not understand.'

After a five-minute silence he tried again.

'What would you like to do this afternoon? Go to a movie?'

'Go home and clean house. Always clean house on Saturday afternoon.'

'Can't you make an exception this once?'

'No reason to make exception.'

'I think there is.'

'What reason?'

He said, exasperated: 'It's customary when a man asks a girl out to lunch on a Saturday for her not to just eat and run.'

'Very silly custom.'

'Hanako-san, listen to me . . .'

He was interrupted by the appearance of a middle-aged Japanese in a battered felt hat and threadbare suit who stopped at the table and stood glowering at Hanako out of narrow, outraged eyes.

'*Americajin no jofu nanka ni natte ii to omou no ka!*' He leaned forward until his nose almost touched hers. '*Baikokudome!*' he rasped, and spat in her face.

Joe jumped to his feet and swung at the man, who ducked, and disappeared behind the inimitable Japanese curtain into the impenetrable sanctum beyond. The manager and boy-san followed close on his heels. They wanted no trouble with the foreigner.

Hanako sat quite still in her chair, her head bent over the table, her hands pressed tight to her eyes.

'What in God's name is going on!' Joe demanded. 'Do you know that bastard? I should have knocked his block off!'

She did not answer, and he thought that she was crying. Then he had remembered he had never seen a Japanese cry, no matter how tragic the circumstances, and he asked: 'What did he say to you? Why did he spit in your face?'

She lowered her hands, and though there were no tears in her eyes, he could see she was crushed, utterly demoralized.

'He call me a whore,' she whispered.

'I'll break his bloody neck! Why do you take any notice of him? He's just a nut.'

'He speak truth. I should not be here with you. You force Hanako to come,' she said bitterly.

Now Joe became angry.

'You're not a whore. You know it and I know it. So what have you got to worry about? You're not a coward. You should stand up to these stupid people – tell them where to get off. I'm not the only American in Japan, and you're not the only girl who's been out with one. It's true we've only been in this country a short time, but we're going to stay a while, so you might as well get used to being seen with us. Hell, we're people. We're human beings.'

She toyed with her chopsticks in silence. Then she pushed away her plate, and without glancing up, said: 'Come with me, please. I show you why Japanese take offence, why they angry at police for not putting prostitute girl in prison . . .'

'But you're not a prostitute!'

'Japanese men think any girl who go with foreigner is prostitute. No excuse for behaviour, however poor, hungry, homeless. Now please come,' she repeated. 'We take street-car to Fukagawa where I lived with Father and Mother – where I was born.'

They stood on the bridge across the Sumida River looking at the waste that was once the industrial suburb of Tokyo, where only a few months before carpenters pulled at their saws, factories blew smoke to the sky, and the dye from the chemical plants painted the canals green as leaves. Now, as far as the eye could see there was nothing – or nearly nothing – a few burnt-out wooden frames, twisted iron girders, sewage pipes scattered over the parched ground like jack-straws dropped from heaven.

This was what the B29 bombers had done, he thought – ten thousand little incendiaries after high explosives had screamed through the bomb-bay doors. Thumbs up and away from the black-red orchids of exploding shells, and the white-hot pistils of the tracer bullets.

Hanako, her face expressionless, spoke in a voice so low he could barely hear her:

'I was at Ginza movie with my friend Tamiyo. When we left very late the siren rang, but we pay no attention because Tokyo raided many times and not much damage. People laugh – say American no good at bomb dropping. I say goodnight to Tamiyo and start home on bicycle when suddenly come big explosion on other side of river. I look up and see planes in wide circle come over and down and up again, rolling on back, engines hammer-hammer, then fly away. Soon sky light up like August fireworks. I think of Father and Mother in house near lumberyard and pedal fast. After one hour cramp in leg make me stop here on bridge. Never see such awful sight. Flames everywhere swept by wind. People with horrid burns standing waist deep in river. I try to run through fire, but soldier grab me. I wait three, four hours until houses all gone. I stop old man carrying scorched bedding and ask about Father and Mother. He shake his head – say everyone killed. I not believe him, break away, and run through streets, past ladies with burned babies at breast, past little children, all dead, crouched together like charcoal sticks . . . '

'Hanako, stop it!' Joe said. 'That's enough. You don't have to tell me any more. I understand it. It must have been ghastly!'

She recited her nightmare tonelessly.

'I try to reach home near primary school. Streets all broken – no streets at all. Pass school and see bodies of children who ran to their teachers for help. Two thousand lie face down on scorched concrete floor, kimonos still smoking. Teachers, too.'

'Hanako, please!'

She walked slowly forward: 'Come, I show you my house – where I lived.'

He followed her reluctantly across the waste-land. But now, with the coming of dusk, he saw that the area was not deserted. People were clustered in potholes and bomb craters over small bonfires, seeking protection from the cold. As they approached what looked like a long, empty tunnel, a boy hobbled up to them. He wore flapping brown rags and canvas sneakers. His thin, pale face jerked with nervousness as he poled along on a stick, dragging his crippled right leg. A brass can dangled from a rope that held up his trousers; he had to keep both hands on the pole to walk.

He spoke to Hanako, then led them to the gaping tunnel which, to Joe's surprise, turned out to be crowded with people: emaciated, pot-bellied children naked but for their torn pants and sandals; old men in tatters of cloth, filthy bandages wrapped about their feet; mothers clutching their wizened babies, their tiny eyes wide with fright.

'Jesus!' breathed Joe. 'What is this? Who are they?'

'This was Father's lumberyard. Many worked for him. Nowhere to go now.'

One or two old people raised their heads and bowed to Hanako, but others paid them no attention, only huddled closer to the fire as if afraid the newcomers would try and push past them to get near the warmth.

Outside the tunnel a very old man lay on his back. He was dressed in a ripped undershirt and shorts through which his wrinkled brown skin showed. His eyes stared blankly at the sky, and as Joe watched he saw his jaw drop. Several people jumped up and bent over him. They tried to lift him, but could not, and dragged him into the tunnel. Others ahead cleared a path to the fire. They looked at the old man, talking in low voices, then one of them bent down and started to strip him, passing the rags from hand to hand to those at the back who could not reach the fire. Joe stepped forward, but Hanako restrained him. When the old man was completely naked, Hanako turned away.

They left the tunnel and walked on in silence for a few hundred yards. Finally Hanako stopped before a heap of rubble, and bowed her head.

'This is my home,' she said softly. 'When I found it soldiers were taking Father and Mother away. They lifted the bodies with a big hook and put them in truck. The burned flesh' – she stifled a sob – 'the burned flesh pulled away . . .'

'Hanako,' Joe whispered. 'Hanako . . .'

She turned and buried her face in his chest.

They sat at a small table in the Tokyo Station bar awaiting the departure of Hanako's train for Kamakura.

'A jug of *sake*,' he told the boy-san. And to Hanako: 'We can both use it. That was quite a harrowing experience.'

She did not reply. He said: 'Now you've convinced me, it's only fair to tell me more.'

'More?'

'About yourself – your parents – your marriage.'

'What use to tell?'

'I'll decide that. We'll begin with your father. He owned a lumberyard in Fukagawa. He must have been a rich man.'

'Not rich – not poor. Had hard time as student. No money for school or university. But he was good looking with fine brain. Marriage was arranged to my mother who came from upper middle-class family in Tokyo. Mother only child, so Father took Mother's name, also family lumber business.'

'I get it. And was your marriage arranged too?'

'*Hi*. Shiro-san, eldest son of noble Kyoto family. His cousin's daughter was classmate at Christian School in Yokohama 1942. Morimoto family wanted grandchild because Shiro-san was naval officer in dangerous South Sea waters and might be killed, leaving no heir. Cousin took my photograph to Morimoto-san who liked it.' She blushed, sipping her *sake*. 'I wore special kimono that day. If not, maybe never get married.'

'I don't think it had anything to do with the kimono,' Joe grinned.

'Meeting arranged in Kyoto and quick marriage performed while Shiro-san was on leave. One month later he was lost in wreck of transport off New Guinea. Nine months later my daughter Naoko was born.'

'Did you love your husband?' Joe asked.

'How I know? One week, that's all. Always drunk on *sake*. Beat me because he hated war, hated transport, hated South Sea. Not my fault Japan attack China, Pearl Harbor.'

'Poor Hanako. But you got along all right with your in-laws?'

'What?'

'Your family. Your new family.'

'Never. Very strict Buddhists. How you say – proud, narrow-minded. Never forgive Hanako because she attend Christian School. Never let me speak English in house. Japanese won't learn foreign language. And think foreigner who speak Japanese up to some trick – want to intrude on privacy. In old days father-in-law wouldn't have Hanako for daughter.'

'Why not, for God's sake?'

'Not born into noble family. Until Father marry Mother, he worked in factory. In old days everyone must fit into proper pigeon-hole. Obey, or give orders. Two different worlds. Peasants not permitted to eat white rice. Merchants must have small house in suburb. Farmers not permitted to cover floor with *tatami* – must sit on bare earth. Now things much better.'

'Then you do get along with your in-laws.'

'Never. They expect dowry from my father. Also kimonos, bedding, furniture like most brides bring to husband's house, but lumberyard lose money after war began and Father not afford it. After my husband's death my family-in-law, who never accept me from the beginning, made things very difficult. I leave and take job at Meijiya on Ginza.'

'And your daughter? Does she live with you in Kamakura?'

'Wouldn't let me have her.'

'That's ridiculous! How could they stop you?'

'Morimoto-san very powerful man. Make things bad for me. They bring up Naoko as strict Buddhist. Because I left on my own accord they say I desert Naoko and law on their side if I take to court. I guess they're right – couldn't look after her under present circumstances, or give good education.'

'But you can see her, can't you?'

'Never. It makes me very sad.'

'It's all so complicated, isn't it?'

'*Hi*. Japan very stupid sometimes.'

'Oh?' With a feeling of relief Joe began to suspect that Hanako might be human after all, if only because of the *sake* – that she wasn't as prejudiced or as anti-American as she tried to make out. 'Like what?' he asked.

She laughed. It was the first time he had heard her laugh, and it rang in his ears like wind bells on a soft summer night.

'Like squatting on heels on *tatami* which stops circulation and stunts growth. Like wearing tight kimono which flattens chest and causes TB. Like carrying babies strapped to back which gives them bow-legs. Like wasting whole day at tea ceremony because ancestor said good for discipline. Like walking one, two miles to smell perfume of cherry blossom, paying no attention to odious *benjo* at home.'

It was Joe's turn to laugh, and when he had done so heartily, he said: 'You know something, Hanako – I don't believe you hate foreigners or the Western way of life as much as you pretend.'

'Perhaps not,' she said, smiling. 'We're told all Americans are demons. You're not demon, Barrett-san.'

'The name is Joe,' he said. 'Well, I wouldn't be too sure. Don't make up your mind yet. We must meet again. How about tomorrow?'

'I must clean house. My friend Tamiyo will come and help.'

'Then next Saturday – same time, same place.'

They were interrupted by the screaming of the loudspeaker. The train for Kamakura was about to leave.

57

'Not Shimbashi Station. People stare and call me whore.'

'Then meet me at one o'clock at the Press Club in Marun-ouchi. I'll be waiting in the bar.'

'Perhaps.'

'Not perhaps. Promise me you'll be there.'

'I promise.'

He helped her on with her coat, then stood and watched her as she ran through the station to the stiles, a slim, graceful figure in a tweed coat and flat-heeled shoes, her dark tresses swirling about her shoulders.

At the entrance to the stiles she paused, turned back, waved, and was gone.

Chapter Seven

The clock above the bar struck one-fifteen. Any minute Hanako should come through the door. Several times the idea had occurred to Joe that she would not come, but each time he put the thought aside.

The lobby was practically empty, the younger reporters having gone to the air base to play football, the older men to Hayama to sail their boats. Among the few remaining at the club was Scott Greenway. To Joe's surprise, he was sitting at a table with a Japanese lady drinking black coffee.

He did not know why he was surprised that Scott should have a date with a Japanese. He had never seen him with her before, and yet it was obvious they were well acquainted, for they sat close together and talked in low, animated voices. She was not young, or in any way typical of the girls who frequented the club. She looked about the same age as Scott, with a touch of grey at the roots of her dark brown hair, and she wore a subdued, brocade, ceremonial kimono. On her lap lay a copy of an English Grammar, which suggested to Joe that she might be a teacher at one of Tokyo's universities.

The clock showed one-thirty, and then a quarter to two. Hanako did not come. Joe was more annoyed than disappointed. She had broken her promise, and now the whole day stretched ahead, empty. Well, he told himself, that was that – the last of Hanako. But even as he spoke the words, he knew it could not be so.

Scott and his friend got up from the table, and as they passed the bar Scott called out that they were on their way to the Kabuki. The lady smiled, and bowed, and Joe felt a wave of warmth sweep over him, as if for a moment he shared their comradeship and intimacy. And then they were gone, leaving him more lonely and sad than ever.

He paid for his drink with a chit and strode to the door. There, coming towards him in a rush of penitence, her coat flying, her hair in disarray, was Hanako! She almost fell into his arms in her haste, stammering her apologies, how she had been held up at the store, how the street-cars were crowded, how she couldn't find the club. All his anger disappeared as he held her slender body tight to him, aware only of the fragrant, musky scent of her hair, and the touch of her cool fingers on his hand.

'It's all right,' he said, laughing. 'There's nothing to get excited about. You're here – that's what matters.'

'Joe-san, please forgive Hanako . . .'

'Hanako! So you've broken your promise, Barrett-*san*! I might have expected it. A pretty pair, I must say!'

Joe turned and faced an infuriated Jane Conway standing in the hall, a stack of magazines under her arm.

'Hello. I thought you didn't work on Saturdays,' he said.

'Obviously!'

'Miss Conway – I'd like you to meet Hanako Morimoto.'

'I'm sure you would. But I have no intention of doing so. Or of ever speaking to you again, Joe Barrett!'

Hanako bowed. 'So sorry. I intrude. I go home now to Kamakura.'

'Just do that little thing. And if I were you I wouldn't show your face in here again. There's a board meeting next week to

59

keep you Japs in your place. That means on the Ginza – not in this club.'

Joe said, white-faced: 'I don't think you have much say about that, Miss Conway. You're only the librarian here.'

'That's what you think. The Army requisitioned these premises and they truck in the hamburgers and the liquor, not to mention the vegetables. You know what I mean by *vegetables*.' She looked straight at Hanako. 'They're not grown in your sewers, or fertilized with your stinking honey pots. They come from the good old USA.'

Joe took Hanako's arm, and said quietly: 'Come, we'll be late for lunch.'

As they headed towards Shimbashi, Hanako said: 'Miss Conway good friend?'

'Not particularly.'

'She must care for you a great deal to hate me so.'

'She's crazy. Don't pay any attention to what she said.'

'I must pay attention or will never learn about democracy.'

Her words embarrassed him, and his embarrassment was not in any way diminished when they passed the sidewalk snack bar of the PX in the Hattori Building at Tokyo's busiest crossing where hot dogs and Coca-Cola were sold to the Americans, while the little street children who clustered around received none. He found it ironic that the American Army, enforcing democracy, should be so undemocratic, but Hanako did not seem to notice, or if she did, accepted it as quite proper. And again, when they reached the Daiichi Hotel where Joe had engaged a table for lunch, the great delicacy in which a sign avoided the word Japanese in stating: INDIGENOUS PERSONS NOT PERMITTED TO USE THE ELEVATORS, apparently was completely lost to her.

But not to Joe. He stopped in his tracks, took her arm, and led her into the street.

'To hell with Tokyo,' he said. 'It's a lovely day – let's get out of town – take a train somewhere.'

'Somewhere?'

'Wherever you like. Sometime I want to visit the Lake

60

District, but that's too far. There's Nikko – but that's too cold. How about Atami?'

'Oh, yes!' she said, delighted. 'It will be lovely there. The sun will be warm and the plum trees in bloom.'

'Then Atami it is,' he said, and gave her a hug.

On the train they had a snack of rice balls dressed with sea-weed, then settled back and watched the chequerboard fields fly past, backed by the peaked mountains in the distance where big stone Buddhas sat eyeing them with all-knowing smiles chiselled on their lips. Hanako bubbled over with a sort of secret happiness and could hardly sit still, and yet she kept looking at Joe to see if he were comfortable or bored, or if there was anything she could do for him. It was a new experience for him, because his marriage had left him to expect little from a woman's companionship except continuous bickering and exorbitant demands.

After three hours they reached the little station on the sea front, and emerged into the bright sunshine. The plum trees were in bloom, the cherry and orange trees bursting with buds. The breeze from the sea was fresh and warm. They walked gaily down the curving street to the town, where they spent an hour exploring the shops. Joe bought a wooden *kokeshi* in the shape of a fox, a red lantern swinging at his side. Hanako bought a pair of sandals and nylons, but she wouldn't let him pay for them, or for anything else. He wanted to buy her a garland of flowers in one of the shops, but she said it wasn't lucky and bought it herself, placing it on her hair and dancing around as if it were a tiara of diamonds.

Later they climbed the steep hill overlooking the town where Hanako said there was a Shinto shrine. The narrow path widened after half an hour to allow for the rows and rows of stone lanterns on each side that led finally to an open wooden hut guarded by two tall pines twisted into the shape of a *torii*. Hanging from the pillars was a cluster of straw ropes and small strips of rice paper; on the altar lay a mirror, a sword, and a stone, symbols of Kami, in turn a symbol of the splendour and veneration of Hanako's honourable ancestors.

61

Stepping forward, Hanako reached out her hand and pulled the prayer rope attached to a ponderous gong above their heads. The soft round sounds echoed and re-echoed about the walls. Bowing her head, she clapped her hands three times. 'I'm here, Okami-Sama! Please give welcome to honourable Barrett-san.'

They both stood in silence listening to the sounds fade slowly away, and in that silence, for one blinding, surprising instant, Joe came into direct contact with the heart and mind of Japan, became a living part of its beauty and its grandeur – sensed, however blindly, the rich secret of its inscrutability.

And then the revelation passed, and he found himself staring down at the altar with its cracked mirror, its sword, its stone, and wondered how Hanako could accept these mundane symbols as anything connected with the Supreme Being, any more than he could accept the fact that the badgers and bears of Japan were His divine attendants who assumed human forms, healed the sick, guarded against evil, and predicted the future.

On the way back to town he asked her.

'I don't want to belittle your faith, Hanako – we all have our beliefs and disbeliefs – but can you really accept those symbols back there as anything to do with Kami? That cracked mirror . . . ?'

'I don't know,' she replied. 'When we have face-ache we come here and ask help, pray for child or for brother in war. Is it any different in America? Christian school say wine and bread are symbols there.'

'Well, I wouldn't say . . . '

'Why say? What use? Perhaps Hanako mistaken about Kami. Perhaps everyone mistaken. So what does it matter if I pray to mirror or stone as long as I pray?'

'You've got something there,' he grinned, and did not speak again until they entered the town.

The afternoon had been so enjoyable that Joe dreaded the moment when Hanako would suggest it was time to leave. So he was delighted when she stopped in front of the Fuji-ya Hotel and said: 'Atami famous for hot springs. You like to take bath?'

'I sure would,' he replied, brushing the dust from his coat and trousers.

'Come, then. We take room at hotel and change.'

It was a beautiful hotel on three floors, its front windows facing the sea. A servant met them and took their shoes and gave them cloth slippers in exchange. Then they crossed to the desk where the manager was standing. He bowed and said: 'Very hoppy have American guest. Sign, please,' and pointed to the book.

Joe blushed, feeling awkward and embarrassed sharing a room with Hanako, if only to change in, but when he looked at her she seemed quite calm, and picking up the pen, he wrote: 'Mr Joe Barrett and guest'. The manager bowed again, then let them down the hall to a big airy room with nothing in it except straw mats on the floor and a low table on the balcony.

Joe did not know what to think or do. Here he was alone with Hanako in an hotel room in Atami, yet she had never once let him hold her hand. He thought he would never understand how Japanese girls felt about things, or how their minds worked. But then Hanako took over, swiftly sliding back the *fusuma* and producing two kimonos which she explained belonged to the hotel, and which they were supposed to wear to the bath and for the rest of the evening. She put one on before slipping out of her dress, then excused herself and went into the corridor.

Joe slipped off his clothes and put on the other kimono. There were two sections to it, one cotton and one silk, with a big sash. He found difficulty in getting it around his waist, and had just managed it when Hanako returned.

She took one look at him and burst out laughing. 'Excuse, please. Kimono inside out,' and before he could prevent it, she pulled the sash and snatched the kimono off, leaving him standing stark naked in the middle of the room.

He tried to snatch it back, to cover himself, but Hanako smiled, rearranged it, slipped it over his shoulders, then tied the sash with the expertise of a conjurer.

'Silly boy-san,' she said. 'You embarrassed because I see you naked? What you do in bath when twenty–thirty people see?'

He remembered his experience in the bath at Beppu, and said: 'Oh. You mean it's that kind? You don't mind?'

'Why should I? Many people in Japan. Very few baths. But here many baths. If you like private bath we take private bath.'

'You mean you and I – together?'

'What you want? American bath? No American bath in Japanese hotel.'

He took a deep breath, said: 'I'm game. I was only thinking of you. I thought . . .'

'Very silly thought. I scrub your back and give you massage. Miss Conway give you massage?'

'My good God, no,' he said, and laughed, unable even to picture it.

He followed her down the corridor and through a door that led into a high-ceilinged room, one side of which consisted of a large, single pane of glass overlooking the sea. Beneath the glass a deep, blue-tiled pool ran the length of the room, then curved back to a rocky waterfall steaming with hot spring water.

They slipped off their kimonos, and stood for a moment looking at each other, smiling. Although Joe was prepared for a shock, he had not anticipated the exquisite body of this girl of Asia who stood before him in all her glory like a strand of gold against the blue of the sea, her large eyes smiling into his, her jet-black hair cascading down her back. The steam rising from the pool was an embellishment and made her seem more robust than she looked in her clothes. Her legs were long and beautifully formed, her breasts full and gently pointed. She was lovelier than he had ever imagined a woman could be.

Surprisingly, he found that he felt no embarrassment about himself, only confidence that his body was straight-limbed, without a flaw, or appeared to be in her eyes, for she said happily: 'You are very handsome man, Joe-san. I never before see white skin like you. You don't mind yellow skin?'

'Not yellow. Ivory. An ivory figurine. You're the most beautiful woman I've ever seen!'

He then took her by the wrist and started to lead her to the pool, but she, in turn, led him to a corner of the room where there were two small wooden stools and a bucket of water.

'Wash first,' she said, handing him a cake of soap and a cloth the size of a pocket handkerchief.

They sat down side by side, soaping themselves and alternately dousing themselves with water from the bucket.

'Is this necessary?' Joe asked. 'You mean to say you have to sit here like this and scrub your bottom in full view of the bathers in the communal pool?'

'Japanese don't bathe in own dirty water like Miss Conway.'

Joe said, provoked: 'Will you please stop talking about Miss Conway. I've told you she means nothing to me.'

'You not take bath with Miss Conway?'

'Never.'

'You . . . no, not fair question. I put other way. You love American girl' – she pointed to her breast – 'with heart?'

'Absolutely not!' And then seriously: 'I don't think I've ever been in love, Hanako. In fact, I know I haven't. I've known many girls. I've been married, as you have . . .'

'You mean . . . ?'

'I mean what I say. I *have* been married. It's all over and done with. I know I've never been in love because I've never felt – well – the way I have today, just fooling about this town with you, and the way I feel now sitting on this damned uncomfortable stool with this ridiculously inadequate towel, facing the most beautiful, the most maddening person I've ever known!'

'You very crazy American,' she laughed. 'Now we take bath and catch train home before something terrible happens.'

'Terrible?'

'You come now,' she said, and pulled him off the stool.

Back in their room, their bodies glowing like steamed scampi after their hot bath, Joe took Hanako in his arms, and said: 'Do we have to go back to Tokyo tonight? Tomorrow is Sunday, and . . .'

They were interrupted by the entrance of a maid who came in on her knees, a tea tray held aloft in her hands. She shuffled across the *tatami* and put the tray on the table on the balcony, then returned, slid back the *fusuma*, removed the bed rolls and a paper-shaded night lamp from the shelf, and placed them on the floor. Then she backed out again on her knees.

'Well, that settles that!' Joe grinned.

And then suddenly he grinned no more. They stood facing each other, staring silently into each other's eyes.

Outside a great red moon had come out of the sea and hung over them, turning Hanako's hair into flame, and just beneath the window came one of the sweetest sounds Joe had ever heard: the faint note of a flute played by a noodle vendor as he pushed his belled cart along the beach.

'Hanako?'

'Yes?'

'Hanako – are you real?'

'Very real,' she laughed.

And then suddenly she was tight against him, her arms about his neck, her body close and supple and clinging, her mouth against his, the soft firmness of her breasts against his chest. She was laughing and drawing him tighter, and then suddenly her body was no longer soft and supple, but tense and fierce and tight-locked. And where there had been laughter there was laughter no longer, but a breath of a sigh deep down, and where there had been words coming, there were no words, only lips that quivered, groping for words.

He picked her up in his arms and carried her silently to where the bed rolls were laid together on the floor. He put her down on the quilts, then crossed to the balcony and slid the wooden screen over the windows, shutting out the world. He came back and knelt beside her saying nothing, and she looked up at him gravely, then smiled, and gently pulled him down beside her.

Chapter Eight

They sat on the balcony by the open window breakfasting on whitebait, rice, sour berries, bean soup, and pickles. For half an hour before the maid had entered with the tray, Joe had sat propped on the bedroll watching Hanako brushing her slippery hair which he had tangled beyond recognition during the hours she had slept in his arms, a smile playing about her mouth and eyes, and now, still aglow with her warmth, he asked:

'We have the whole day before us, Hanako. What would you like to do?'

'I'm just happy to be here – to serve your pleasure in any- thing you want to be done.'

'As if you haven't already! How can I tell you how happy you've made me? What is your secret? I wish I knew.'

'Secret? There is no secret to love. You love or you not love. You make me happy, too, after long time living alone.'

'Then you mean what you say?'

'Mean?'

'That you'll serve my pleasure in whatever I want done?'

'Yes, I say. Why you question Hanako?'

'I would like to meet your daughter. We're nearly a third of the way to Kyoto. We don't have to be back until late tonight. We can take her to lunch . . .'

She put down her chopsicks, and once again her face became tense, her attitude defensive, her eyes almost hard.

'No, it is not possible. I told you Morimoto-san won't let me come to house . . .'

'But you were sitting together at the trial. He didn't seem such an ogre then.'

'It is different. As a family I must put on show to public. It is custom. But I'm not welcome in the house.'

'But your daughter lives there! You have every right to see her. You're not a coward. Sometime you'll have to face up to them.'

'I am coward,' she said.

'I don't believe it. And to prove it we're going to Kyoto and take your daughter to lunch.'

Her eyes softened, and she smiled faintly, looking through the window at the sea.

'You speak as if Naoko big girl with big appetite. She only one year old!'

Joe laughed, and reached for her hand.

'I suppose it's because I keep thinking of her in terms of you. Does she look like you?'

'How do I know? She has legs and arms and eyes and nose, and black hair like all Japanese children.'

'I'm sure she's exceptional. Anyway, we're going to find out. If you're afraid of Morimoto, I'm not. The least he can do is to throw us out.'

She was silent, and then she said: 'Every day after lunch *uba*, breast-feeding mother, sit with Naoko in garden. We go and hide in bushes and you can see daughter, yes?'

'Okay, we go. But I won't guarantee we'll hide in the bushes. We'll play it by ear. Get ready and I'll go down and pay the bill. I'll meet you at the front door.'

The ancient capital of Kyoto was a relief after Tokyo. No pathetic little kids in rags scampered around the slop cans; nobody fished in filthy canals; nobody gardened or weeded in burnt-out patches of ground. There was no lingering smell of death, no feeling of pain or horror.

Hanako led Joe through the quiet streets, squared like a chess-board beneath the blue-black mountains of Hiei and Higashiyama, past buildings staggering in their unfamiliarity. She pointed out to him the Palace with its wide moats flanked by trees, the great wooden gates, the temples double-roofed with Japanese cypress bark, the corners upswept in Chinese style. Doves fluttered out from behind the eaves, then perched on the stone lanterns or vanished into the haze which somehow gave the city a feeling of grace and tranquillity.

As three o'clock was the time Hanako suggested they visit her daughter, they had a snack across the street from the market where they watched the wooden carts with their hitched oxen backing into the stalls containing slabs of meat and tubs of fish. Later they crossed the Kamo River to Gion and walked down a street lined with squat wooden houses with smooth façades and individually carved front doors which Hanako explained was the geisha distinguishing mark. They were lucky to find one door ajar, and looked in. They caught a glimpse of a long passage with its highly polished floor stretching away to rooms with sliding screens facing on to the back garden where the sound of running water mingled with the soft strains of a *shamisen*. A dancing girl in a multi-coloured silk kimono, her classical whitewashed face mask-like beneath her dark *shimada* hair-do, fluttered past and disappeared in the shadows. High-pitched cackles and the scent of hot *sake* drifted through to them, and then the door suddenly snapped shut, and a completely alien and fascinating world faded from Joe's sight, if not from his memory.

From a shop not far away they rented two bicycles and pedalled out towards the north part of the city to the foot of Kinugasa Hill, surrounded by ancient temples and shrines tucked away in beautifully landscaped gardens and wooded parks. It was like entering a new era, untouched by war, an era of the past when Emperor Kanmu and the succeeding emperors dwelt in the city venerated as gods, living out their lives in traditional though rigid splendour.

Finally they drew up before a huge gate, but before Joe could dismount, Hanako beckoned him to follow her. They continued along the length of a high fir hedge until she slipped off her bicycle, concealing it in the surrounding brush. He placed his beside hers, and they crept back to the hedge, searching for a gap in the firs where they could peer into the garden. After a few minutes of groping about with her hands, Hanako beckoned to him again, then held a finger to her lips.

Behind the hedge an enclosed Japanese garden stretched away level with the floor of the house and the parted *shoji*, so it appeared to be an integral part of it. There was a rock pool dotted with pink lotus blossoms, stunted, twisted pines with their green leaves growing in the clean white sand, carefully

69

trimmed shrubbery backed by tall maple trees, and, beyond, the soaring mountain range.

Sitting on a stone bench beside the pool was the Nanny, reading a magazine. Beside her stood a baby carriage, and in the carriage an unrecognizable apparition bundled in woollens, a silk coverlet wrapped around it, the head crowned by a knitted woollen cap.

'What *is* it?' Joe whispered.

'My daughter, Naoko,' she said breathlessly. 'I'm happy she look so well.'

'Are you crazy? You can't even see her face!'

'I not need to. I carry her picture always in my heart.'

'Well, I don't. I want to get a look at her. I should think you would, too, after all this time.'

'No, I've seen. I'm content. We go now, Joe-san, please!'

'Not on your life. Come on,' he said, and started to drag her through the hedge.

She broke away, and was about to run for her bicycle when, as if by an act of God, the Nanny dropped her magazine and stood up. Walking quickly over the carefully placed stepping stones, she disappeared behind the house.

'Hanako!' Joe cried hoarsely. 'Come quick! Your *uba* has gone for her tea break! Now's our chance!'

She crept up beside him, deftly parting the branches, then grasping his hand, led him, trembling, to the baby carriage.

Sweeping all caution aside, she picked her daughter up in her arms, slipped off the woollen cap, and hugged her to her breast.

Joe looked at the child and saw a tiny flower face, chubby and round, large black eyes, a button nose, and a tuft of stiff black hair which rose straight into the air like a Fuller brush. As she clung to her mother, her off-shaped head lolled as if her neck were a broken stalk. She was the most fascinating little creature he had ever seen.

'*Doshite kokoe irashai mashitaka, Hanako-san. Ikenaikoto gozonji desho.*'

Joe looked up, and recognized the speaker at once – recognized the distinguished Japanese with his long, pale, ascetic face and grey beard standing just inside the parted *shoji* dressed

70

as he had first seen him in an elegant dark kimono stamped with the family crest. Before Joe could gather his wits, Morimoto continued: '*Kono katawa daredesuka?*'

Hanako, who had replaced her daughter in the carriage, was bowing so low she could not have replied had she wished to. Joe understood Morimoto's last words, demanding to know who he was, and said: 'I hope you'll forgive us for intruding, Mr Morimoto. You must not blame Hanako-san for our visit. It was my suggestion. I wanted to see the child. My name is Joe Barrett – a friend of Hanako's.'

Morimoto looked pained. Obviously he did not wish to converse in English, and recalling Hanako's explanation, Joe almost felt pity for the man faced with a dilemma not of his choosing. Joe was a foreigner – worse, an American, a symbol of his shame – the shame that his oldest son should die, not by his own hand, honourably, but in dishonour, miserably in the South Seas; and the younger son, just as loved, a captive of the Americans, who in a short time would be hung by the neck until dead.

And yet Morimoto was an intelligent and cultured man, and his strict code of discipline and etiquette forebade him from showing the slightest discourtesy to a visitor, uninvited as he was.

'You will join us for tea, Mr Barrett,' he said, bowed, and re-entered the house.

A maid appeared and exchanged their shoes for felt slippers. They followed Morimoto over the shining cream *tatami* into a long corridor of polished boards lined with a priceless collection of black ink paintings and colour drawings into another spacious room bare except for its waxed ceiling planks, scroll, and vase of flowers. The maid placed three cushions on the *tatami*, one in front of the *tokonoma*, the seat of honour, then withdrew.

'*Dozo*,' Morimoto said, motioning to Joe.

He sat cross-legged on the cushion while Hanako and her father-in-law squatted upon their heels in front of him.

Morimoto bowed. Joe and Hanako bowed.

'Welcome to my house. You have come to see my son Shiro's

71

daughter. Why did you not come to the door, Mr Barrett, so I could have welcomed you?'

'I understood we wouldn't be welcome.'

'I am speaking of you, sir. You say *you* wished to see my grand-daughter?'

'That's right. And so did Hanako. She hasn't seen her for some time. She would not come by herself, thinking she's not welcome here. Can that be possible – you refuse to let Hanako visit her own daughter?'

'Please, I must explain . . .'

Taken aback by the interruption, Mr Morimoto caught his breath. Obviously he was deeply offended by Hanako's outburst, expecting her to remain silent in his presence, and her interference in his carefully planned examination of his guest shocked and angered him. And then, as if realizing from past experience that such a hope was futile where Hanako was concerned, he smiled indulgently and withdrew his fan from the folds of his sash.

'I have spent much time considering what is best both for my grand-daughter and for her mother, Mr Barrett. I have reached the conclusion that it would only bring pain and unhappiness if communication were to be resumed.'

'But she is Naoko's mother! Surely she has as much right to her as you have.'

Morimoto waved his fan, and said impatiently: 'I see you do not understand our traditions, Mr Barrett. My eldest son has been killed in the war. My grand-daughter must bear the responsibility of carrying on the family name. She will inherit my house and my estate, and when she is of age she will marry a man of my own choosing. She will live here and will be raised strictly in the tradition of our faith and so honour our ancestors' spirits who will guide her in the future in spite of our present misfortune.'

'You are saying that her own mother has no choice in the matter? Has no claim to the child whatever?'

'That is correct. She has left the house of my son to live and work in Tokyo. It was her decision and, if I may presume, the fact that she has seen fit to associate with a foreigner is proof enough that my worst fears have been confirmed. I do not know who you are, sir, or how well you know my daughter-in-law, but I tell you in all honesty that a member of the family of Morimoto would not defy our traditions as Hanako has done. And if she were to have access to her daughter, would she not allow the child to be as permissive as herself? Even encourage her to marry an Occidental, become a spiritually misplaced person?'

'Would that be such a tragedy?' Joe said angrily.

'Have I not explained to you?' Morimoto replied sharply. 'Our family chooses to remain true to ourselves in reverence of our race. My son, if he were alive, would see treason in his daughter giving birth to children who were not of our racial stock . . . '

They were interrupted by the maid who served them tea. Hanako sipped hers dutifully without glancing up. Joe pushed his cup aside in a moment of pique, suddenly finding Mr Morimoto's venerable presence and his aristocracy suffocating.

After an interval of silence, Morimoto replaced the fan in the folds of his sash. 'You have heard of Prince Konoye, Mr Barrett?'

'The former Premier? He committed suicide.'

'Quite right. Because he lost faith in Japan. When you dropped the atomic bomb on Hiroshima he accepted our defeat as irrevocable. Like so many of us, he knew of our victories, but not of our reverses, and our defeat was therefore more crushing because it was unexpected.'

'I don't understand you,' Joe said.

'If I shared Prince Konoye's despair, believed that the Americans had truly won a victory, perhaps I would be forced to view my grand-daughter's welfare in a different light. But I do not share the Prince's anxiety. On the contrary, I believe Japan has a great future because, as a result of your bomb, you have tilted the moral balance of the globe in our favour. Don't misunderstand me. We are not fools. We admire your technical achievement. If we had had the bomb first we would have used it. Total war is total war. You do not put such a devastating weapon in the ground and bury it. Nevertheless, your bomb has

73

rid us of our guilt, atoned for our crimes. We have paid the penalty, and our debts are settled. Now we can return to our earthly Paradise before the apple fell, follow strictly the tradition of the divine age set down to us by the Mikado and his ministers.'

His eyes turned misty, as grey as his beard, and in spite of his annoyance, Joe felt almost pity for the man, lost as he was in the world of the past, living here as in his museum, surrounded by his paintings and his scrolls, his temples and his shrines, the guardians of his thoughts and desires, and therefore his actions.

'You see, Mr Barrett,' he continued, 'our people have been raised like the Sazae seashell which shuts into itself when touched by a ripple of water. We shall no longer permit others to open our shell, or think of battleships and bombs, of which we have had enough, but instead respect our privacy, our loyalty, and our pride, making sure that the ethics in our ancient *shinto* are never breached again.'

He put down his cup, and rose. Obviously the audience was at an end.

Joe struggled to his feet, said: 'I don't believe it will be as easy as all that, Mr Morimoto. This is the second time in a hundred years your country has been opened to the outside world, and I think you can expect some surprises.'

'Perhaps, perhaps.' He shrugged. 'But I do not believe it. Not here in Kyoto, certainly. We shall carry on as our ancestors did before us. And now, sir, you will excuse me.'

'Of course,' Joe said, bowed, and took Hanako's hand.

It was then that he realized the old man had not once addressed or spoken to her during their entire visit.

The long trip back to Tokyo had hardly begun when Hanako, sitting by the window, fell into a deep sleep. Outside rain trickled down the pane. Joe lit a cigarette, thinking how fortunate he was to have an empty seat next to him in which to stretch his legs, when the far door to the carriage opened and a bulky Japanese came tramping down the aisle and occupied it.

Joe looked into a fat face, a fat mouth, a fat chin. The man

74

took off his long black leather gloves, nodded, and said in English: 'Not such good day.'

He pushed his suitcase on to the baggage rack and took off his coat, which he folded and placed beside the suitcase. Joe saw his oval, almost round eyes with their intent pupils. He smiled and said:

'I speak English. Shall we talk a bit?'

He wore some sort of uniform, and Joe became curious.

'I'd like to. A train ride can become quite boring.'

The man put out a fat hand and Joe took it, surprised because it was so soft.

'I am Doigaki,' he said. 'Captain of ex-Imperial Japan Navy.'

The hand lingered long enough for Joe to feel something was wrong with it. He glanced down and saw a scar from a very bad wound. Another scar was even worse. It creased the upper portion of his left cheek, almost to the left eye.

On his dark tunic, over the region of the appendix, was a flat, round, gold medallion inset with rubies. Noticing Joe's interest, Doigaki explained: 'Japan Purple Heart, officer class.'

Joe looked at the uniform. The material was dark blue with a loop of braid over one shoulder. The throat tabs, obviously of rank, consisted of three cherry blossoms in silver on a gold and blue background; the cap had an anchor nestling among the gold leaves. Joe's eyes dropped to his muddy sea-boots.

'My ship *Akitsushima*, flying-boat tender, incorporated several of my unique designs,' he said, speaking straight out, with conceit, but also with composure. 'Never once hit in over fifty assaults by your air arm in Solomons.'

'What happened to the *Aki* . . . to your ship?'

Doigaki snapped his lips. 'Sunk off Mindoro. However, I was no longer in command. My next ship "A" Class cruiser, most dependable. I brought her through much action.'

'Where is she now?'

'Oh, your arm found her at Kure, in Japan Inland Sea. She was damaged and lies awash. I was no longer in command.'

Joe smiled, but Doigaki's face was impassive. He resettled his shoulders, cleared his throat, and waited.

75

Joe broke the silence. The captain answered all his questions briskly. Pearl Harbor? Most surprising development. He had been in North China at the time. But not sneak attack. Japan was poor country, poor people must live by wits. And how about American Fort Sumter? He was student of American history. He had been to America many times. Great nation, but occupation should be brief – year, two year.

Joe probed a bit deeper. Doigaki sniffed: 'Absurd Western fancy. Emperor certainly not god. No Japanese say so. Foreigner not understand Japan Emperor feeling. Emperor father to all his people.' He sighed. 'We are both honest men, sir. Tojo and Japan Army start such foolish war. Now there is peace, must be good peace. Let us both try. Let us reflect critically. Japanese love General MacArthur, for like Emperor he is noble.'

He began to appear tired. After a lengthy pause, Joe asked: 'Captain, one more question. What will you do now?'

He closed his eyes: his hand dropped to his side.

'I have gone to Maizuru,' he said slowly, 'to assist your navy in destruction of remaining elements of mine. Now I return to birthplace. It is in mountains and very beautiful.'

He settled back, his eyes half shut and his chin fat against his collar. The talk was over.

It was raining much harder outside.

Chapter Nine

Spring came to the islands with a rash of cherry and peach blossoms in the parks and roadsides, and in the foothills the melting of the snow had left in its wake the glitter of orange groves and strawberry beds and masses of rose and white azalea. In the shrubberies of the mulberry trees silk cocoons lay spread out in the sunshine on wide flat trays in the back gardens of the little wooden houses tucked away in the forests.

For the Japanese it was floral viewing and festival time — Buddha's birthday and the Emperor's birthday — a slack period in Tokyo for both Joe and Hanako with the exodus of the faithful into the country and to the seaside to participate in the welcome warmth after the cold, depressing winter.

Joe and Hanako eagerly took part in this exodus, Joe grateful for the opportunity to explore the inroads and byways of Japan with a companion who could not only speak the language, but who now accepted him freely and openly as her lover, in spite of the periodic scenes of disapproval displayed by her compatriots.

They spent a weekend at Nara, the birthplace of Japanese art, explored the magnificent palaces and fed the tame deer in the park, and they went to Matsue in Shimane Prefecture to visit Lafcadio Hearn's old residence where he lived while teaching English at the Shimane school. Another weekend they took a train to Gotemba, the gateway village to Fuji and the five lakes. There they hired a motor scooter to take them to Hakone, where Joe had always wanted to go, stopping at the summit of Otome Toge to have tea at a roadside *sake* bar facing the magnificent panorama of the lake walled by its green hills, the smoking solfatara of Ojigoku, and the massive heights of Komagataka, with the distant prospects over the Bay of Sagami to the Pacific.

They did not stay at the big hot springs hotel clinging to the sides of the gorge, its terraces and grounds belching fumes of sulphur, but slept out under the stars in a pine grove at the edge of the lake, pungent with the scent of freshwater and wet fern. They went boating in the morning, and horseback riding in the afternoon, exploring the narrow dirt tracks that wound through the pines coming out at the oddest places: a hill crowned by masses of cryptomeria where they could look down upon the sloping hills to Gotemba, a plateau at the foot of Fuji, so overwhelmingly close that they could see the rest huts that lined the pilgrim roads around the summit. Or they would find themselves, suddenly, back on the shore of the lake. They would climb off their horses and Hanako would press her cool cheek against his lips, her brilliant eyes glowing from their ride, and smiling the little smile he had come to know so well, take his hand and lead him into a silent grove thickly spread with needles. They would undress and lie down together, and he would know again the sweet wonder of her body, as small and exquisite as a child's, and the kisses that her mouth gave which first passed like a wave of harmony through her whole being. There was hunger in their love, but what Joe felt during those days was beyond mere pleasure and desire. It was an awareness of the enormous bond of tenderness that had sprung up between them. He forgot that he was American and she was Japanese. They were simply timeless beings without nation or colour. He saw her only as a woman, more lovely than any he had ever known.

And then they would race down to the village to do their last-minute shopping. The stalls had a good variety of fresh fish and sold almost everything from seeds to rain hats and straw shoes for man and beast. Hanako drew a net bag from her pocket and fell in behind the other women. Joe followed at her side, smiling or shaking his head in answer to her questioning glances when she came upon a particularly appetising or a particularly unappetising concoction spread before them. He couldn't remember ever having gone shopping with a girl before – and certainly not with Caroline, who left such a mundane chore in the hands of the butler – and found that he was enjoying himself immensely. It gave him a warm feeling, almost of possession, to walk beside Hanako and have her suddenly press his hand when she stopped to buy something which her womanly instinct told her was too expensive, or have her flash her eyes at him as if to say: 'Quick, grab it before it's gone', or pucker her mouth, meaning: 'Be careful, it might have worms.' Walking beside her, gaily helping her to tuck their purchases into the bag, he had the odd sensation that this *had* happened to him before, that he had been shopping with a girl, but only this girl, only Hanako.

And then they would return the horses to the stable and run down to the water's edge to cook the trout and the vegetables over a small twig fire. Later they slipped into the cold mountain water and took turns scrubbing each other's back. Sometimes they stayed in the water for over an hour, scrubbing and arguing and laughing, until Joe would lift her in his arms and carry her back to their bed of pine needles where he rubbed her down, kissing her as he clothed her in towels.

On the Emperor's birthday they took a train to Nagoya and changed to a private line for Toba on the Gulf of Ise. The coaches were crowded with village delegates on a pilgrimage to the shrine, and they had to fight their way through the door amid a wild scramble for seats between the most tenacious seat-keepers Joe had ever come across. They fought their way through the seething mob, battered by bulging suitcases, slashed by bundles of blossoming thorn trees and fish crates, and stabbed by umbrellas. They fell upon the hand straps, gasping for breath, while passengers tramped over their feet and children darted between their legs before jumping on to the laps of their parents, wiping their shoes and running noses on whatever clothing was near at hand.

Most of the passengers were villagers engaged in farming, fishing, or diving. The faces of the older people were deeply creased, their dark blue kimonos made from rough hard-wearing cotton cloth. Before the train had hardly pulled out of the station many of them were fast asleep, crouching in kneeling positions on the seat, their hands on the window-sill, their buttocks and clogs thrust into the aisle, their heads bobbing between their knees. Several of the younger men were disorderly or drunk. One particularly unpleasant individual who clung to a strap nearby kept loosening his belt and dropping his trousers to the floor to arrange his underwear, while another tired old fellow who could not push through the crowds to the toilet, urinated on the floor. Half amused, Joe waited for the passengers to do something about it. No one did. They just sat and looked on dispassionately, or pretended to take no notice. The only person who did take offence was Hanako. Her cheeks were flushed with shame.

At Toba they changed again and boarded a bus for Wagu. Darkness had settled over the Gulf, and soon it began to rain. Jagged flashes of blue lightning lit up the curving clay road, which soon turned into a quagmire. It was with a sigh of relief that they finally reached the little pearl-diving village at the mouth of the Gulf facing the narrow straits leading to the Pacific Ocean.

The bus drew up before a small wooden inn tucked away between low fishermen's shacks. Joe hauled their suitcases into the entrance and knocked on the door. It opened a crack and a bewhiskered old lady in a grey kimono inquired what it was they wanted.

'A room for the night,' Joe said.

The woman stared at him as if he had come from Mars. Her glance was neither approving nor disapproving, simply blank with astonishment. Obviously she had never seen an Occidental in her life.

Hanako repeated the request, and they were led to a small five-mat room on the third floor spread with soiled *tatami*. A tiny naked light bulb hanging from the ceiling revealed that two panes were missing from the glass *shoji* which was stuffed with paper, dripping wet from the drenching rain. They were shown the *benjo* where Hanako held her nose, and the communal bath, the water of which was almost black, used as it was by the inn's proprietor, his family, servants, guests, and half the villagers who came to bath and make merry on Saturday nights.

They returned to their room, and while Joe started to unpack, Hanako stared down through the broken *shoji* at the rain-soaked street where the *kumitoriya* was making his rounds from house to house, emptying the *benjos* with his dipper and placing the contents in the honey buckets in the back of his cart. The stench that rose up to greet them was excruciating.

Hanako crossed to him and put her arm about his neck. She was trembling, and there were traces of tears on her cheek – or were they raindrops she had forgotten to wipe away?

'I'm sorry, Joe-san! It was Hanako's idea we come to Ise to see the pearl divers, but it is nasty. We leave now. We take bus back to Toba.'

'Are you crazy?' Joe laughed, kissing her hair. 'There's no bus running this late. And we haven't seen anything of the village yet. Why are you upset?'

'That terrible man on the train – and now this awful place! I'm so ashamed for my country to have such dirty Ryokan . . .' Again she held her nose. 'Such a disgusting *benjo*! Now you know what I mean when I say Japan very stupid sometime. Please, we go, yes?'

'Take it easy, sweetie!' Joe said, emptying the suitcase on to the *tatami*. 'You can't expect perfection in an out-of-the-way village like this. I want to see all of Japan – not just the Imperial Hotel and Tokyo Station. Cheer up and we'll go scouting for something to eat. There must be a *sake* bar nearby where we can get a snack.'

'Don't want to go out in rain,' she said, and sat down on the floor, a determined little figure who had no intention of moving from the room, let alone the hotel, that night.

It was not the first time Joe was to discover this new face to Hanako's character which he had begun to suspect existed, but which he had not encountered before – her stubbornness, her firmness, her readiness to speak her mind. She was not, he found, by any means the down-trodden, patient acceptor which he had come to believe was the chief characteristic of Japanese women.

'But we have to eat,' he reminded her.

She went and closed the shutter, blotting out the night.

'Don't want to eat. Want to go to bed and forget rain and horrible Ryokan.'

'But you're exhausted! Come, take a bath and I'll scrub your back for a change.'

'Don't want bath. Just want you to hold me tight. I show you Hanako not exhausted.' She smiled, and it was as if the rain had suddenly vanished and the sun had broken through the clouds to fill the room with light.

'Okay,' he sighed. He reached for the bottle of Santory he miraculously had thought to put in the suitcase, took a deep swallow, and handed it to her.

She brushed it aside and slipped into his arms, her voice low and husky as she clung to him: 'You all I want, *anata*. Don't need whisky spirit to love you. I love you with all my heart. You show me good American way – not like nasty Japanese man

81

who mess on carriage floor – not like Japanese boys who treat
girls with no respect, like servant. Now, please, we make love,
yes?'

Some time during the early hours of the morning Joe awoke
and lay staring at the ceiling. For a time he could not imagine
where he was. He looked at the wall, expecting to recognize
his surroundings, but saw only the broken shutters which the
first light of dawn struggled to penetrate. Beneath him he could
hear water lapping against wooden pillars, and somewhere, far
in the distance, the high-pitched cry of a gull.

And then slowly the shapes became vague things: his underwear hanging on a hook along with his socks and shirt which
Hanako had washed in the sink in the corridor while he slept,
his toothbrush and razor which she had laid out on the shelf,
and her nude golden body lying curled up next to him.

For a moment Caroline's face came out of the darkness to
haunt him, but it did not remain. It misted, and then died
away, and in its place Hanako filled his vision and his thoughts.

How real and human she was in comparison to the girls he
had known! Lying beside her, the darkness seemed to shimmer
with her presence, hum and come alive. The words that she
had spoken when they were together, locked behind the closed
amado, or walking through the countryside, drifted back to
him, always gentle, never harsh or bitter even when she was
speaking her mind: 'May I, Joe-san? . . . If it is your wish . . . If
it pleases you, *anata*,' instead of the all-too-well-remembered:
'I want . . . I expect . . . Shut up! . . . Go to hell!' Looking down
at her unguarded face, he thought how different it was to the
Western faces he had seen and known – Caroline's, Jane Conway's, the girls he had passed on the streets in Los Angeles and
Santa Barbara which were well made up, efficient, determined,
yet hard and angular and filled with unhappiness – dissatisfied
faces of women who continually complained about their lot,
who asked so much and gave so little, who took an almost
satanic delight in humiliating their men over some trivial affair
for which they had already apologized, if not once, then a
hundred times.

He had known quite a few girls in his time, and knew that in any country there were to be found gentle ones, attractive ones, ugly ones, intelligent ones, brazen and bossy ones. People as a rule were much alike, and yet Hanako had proved an exception to this rule. He didn't know how or why this was so, except that he knew there were girls who were born with an instinct to look after their man, who obviously studied him with the object of making him a happy home, and others who didn't have the desire or the intelligence to do so and ended up with no home at all, and he supposed it was just a matter of chance. He had not thought much about it before, and had taken one girl after another in his stride, but now he was faced with the realization that he had unwittingly stumbled on a rare jewel. And having made this discovery, he found that he did not want to lose her. In fact, he could not imagine himself living without Hanako for one day. In Hanako he had found what he himself had lacked – emotional security, a solid basis for existence. Whether making love to her in an out-of-the-way inn, or in her own little house in Kamakura, or riding horseback with her through the woods, or shopping in the village, without being aware of it they had established a life together as warm, happy, and as complete as was possible for two human beings to do on this earth.

He did not think further than this. It was all too sudden and unexpected. He knew there were questions to be asked and answered – there was the uncertainty of his job – already some of his mates had implied that by going steady with a Japanese girl it could get him into trouble with the powers back home – the child Naoko, and Hanako's own problems with her countrymen's vicious judgement and reproof, but he did not try to answer them and lived, as she did, for the moment.

And yet, for him, it was a moment that encompassed a sense of something wonderful to come – a slow passing from darkness into light. As now, when he lay asleep in their bed by the window, she was there. She was there hidden in his body like the idea of a thing unborn, but which must be born, like the secret awareness of a poem before it was written.

He heard her move on the pillow, felt her eyes were open, and that now she was watching him.

'You no sleep?' he heard her ask.

'No,' he answered.

'Why you not sleep?'

'Because I'm angry with you.'

She sat up straight, covering her breasts with the sheet.

'Why you angry with Hanako?'

'Because you sneaked out of bed and washed my laundry. I've told you not to. A hundred times!'

'It is for women to look after such things,' she laughed. 'Or there'd be no need for us. Now please give Hanako permission to get up. I must open shutters and put on dress.'

Chapter Ten

She slipped from the bed roll and pushed back the shutters while Joe looked on. He caught his breath in surprise. The perfect morning, washed clean and glittering, was mirrored in the calm inlet dotted with fishing boats and long rows of log rafts. Already the little village was humming with activity, the fishermen unloading their catch into tubs on the breakwater while gulls circled with rasping shrieks overhead. The women-folk, too, were far from idle, picking their way among the rocks in the search for crabs in the hollows, unable, it seemed, to relax or tear themselves away for a moment from the secrets of the sea which had been theirs from childhood.

At the end of the harbour stood the pearl farm with its string of sheds stretching to the sea front. Young Ama girls were diving off the shore for oysters in the mother beds. Joe could see them in their bright coloured loincloths flitting back and forth in the calm blue water, their tubs floating about on the surface like flotsam under the sky.

Rather than remain a moment longer in the stuffy little room they went out in search of a café. Eventually they came to an awning where the legs and backs of customers bulged from behind a curtain, and sat down at the counter where they were served a conglomeration of weird sea monsters: octopus, eels, squid, crustacea, and urchins in a large earthen bowl smothered in seaweed.

At the pearl farm they were greeted by the manager, a kindly old man with greying hair and a deeply seamed face, who showed them through the sheds and explained the delicate process of seeding the oysters. They were taken on to the rafts, built of cryptomeria poles lashed together to form a working platform in the centre, and watched the men, naked to the waist, checking the buoys and the tarred barrels upon which the rafts were mounted. They examined the baskets of oysters dangling from their hemp ropes, and spoke to the girls who were scraping the shells clean of barnacles, moss and other marine growths.

They spent the rest of the morning exploring the little coves and beaches, many of them crowded like pebbles with Ama girls warming themselves by brush fires before resuming their diving. Joe walked among them trying not to show his embarrassment at the bare jostling breasts that faced him on all sides, yet unable to take his eyes off the magnificent bodies which had ripened year after year beneath the sun and the sea innocent as the fruits of Eden.

Though she was not an Ama girl, here in this setting by the sea Hanako fitted into the background as if she were one of them, as she fitted into the wooded hills of Hakone, the ancient shrines of Kamakura, the bustle of Tokyo. Sitting beside her staring out over the water he watched her face and saw that it reflected both the sea and the sky – a clear, thoughtful, very beautiful face. But now he saw it was a great deal more than that. He could not explain it exactly, but he was reminded of his revelation at Atami when, for one blinding moment, he had come into contact with the heart and mind of Japan. It was as if the mystery that was nature had so permeated the core of her being that she was a part of the elements which surrounded her. Not only part of the sea and the sky and earth, but also a part of their meaning, embracing, as it were, their desires and capabilities. For him she *was* Japan – all that he had come to know and love about the country. And he did love Japan in spite of its present suffering, its 'quakes and floods and typhoons, its *benjos* and *pachinko* halls.

Without realizing it, almost without his knowledge, his eyes had been opened to the mystery that surrounded the Japanese, so that he sensed, if not yet fully grasped, the secret flash of spirit, the effusion of pity, and the sentiment of nature which bound them in a communion with life. In their sympathy with every living creature – the Japanese believed they were the same essence as beasts – they went about their daily lives with an unaffected simplicity of purpose, having no need or desire to set the world at rights or reduce it to symbols. By sharing their lives as he had with Hanako, the paper homes with their open vistas of the sky, by watching the children at play or a lone woodcutter who had crowned the bundle he carried on his head with a posy of flowers, he had been able to glimpse a truth which he had never before known or experienced, even though he could no more explain it than he could explain the emotion which gripped him after reading a poem of Buson's.

And now, sitting in silence at Hanako's side, her hand in his, he knew quite definitely what he wanted to do, what he would do. Suddenly there were no longer any questions to be asked or answered. Today they had been answered for him.

They chose a table in the village under the trees and ordered a bottle of *sake*. While shopping for souvenirs they had found themselves in front of a store alive with song like a bush and, on entering, had found caged grasshoppers carolling their silver notes while they sucked at slices of cucumber and egg-plant. In a moment of impetuosity Joe had bought one for Hanako, and now they sat with the cage before them, listening to the little creature's endless song.

'Hanako?'

'Yes, Joe-san?'

'Listen to me. Don't speak until I'm finished. Will you promise me that?'

'I promise.'

'Hanako – I want you to marry me. Today – tomorrow – next week – as soon as possible.'

She dropped the little cup she was holding, which fell to the ground, and her face seemed to crumble into a thousand discordant parts, but it was her eyes that summed them all up in a single glance of shock and outrage akin to panic.

'You crazy, Joe! Crazy!' she cried.

'You promised you wouldn't speak until I'd finished.'

'I don't want to hear! You spoil this lovely day! We go now to hotel and pack,' she said, and pushed back her chair.

'Listen to me!' he ordered, and grabbed her by the arm. 'I know it might be difficult for you at first, but you'll get used to it. I'll quit my job on the paper and find permanent work in Japan – a teaching job. There'll be plenty of opportunities to teach English after four years of banning it during the war. I've saved some money – we can buy a house of our own in Kamakura and send for your daughter . . .'

'You crazy! I won't listen, I won't!' she cried, fighting to free herself from his grasp. Finding it impossible, she collapsed in her chair, her hands over her ears.

He rushed on, telling her of his love for her and for Japan, of his unhappy marriage and his rootless, empty, meaningless life in Santa Barbara, not knowing or caring whether she heard him or not, determined to convince her, if not by words, then by sheer force of his resolve that their marriage would succeed because he could not live without her.

When he had finished, she said softly, but with equal determination: 'Thank you, Joe-san, for asking Hanako to marry you. But you not understand. It's impossible in Japan. I'm not strong. I'm coward. I could not bear scorn and filth, the quiet contempt, the hatred of my people. Our children would be foreigner in their own country, outcast, put behind fences with other American children, not wanted or permitted to play with Japanese children. You would come to hate me for being coward. I would hate myself for disgracing the blood of my country. No, I never marry you! But I love you like last night, when you want, if you want, as long as you want.'

87

'You're the one who's crazy!' he said desperately. 'I don't want to have to sneak out of town to be with you. I'm not ashamed of our love, but I want to make a good woman of you, as we say in the States. I want to marry you and be proud of our love.'

'Never!' she said. And then with a wistful smile, infinitely tender, infinitely patient and compassionate: 'It cannot be, Joe-san. But you must not be bitter or feel pity for Hanako. We live by ups and downs, like our houses which fall in earthquake, but which we build again. Nothing ever permament in Japan. We prepared for it, as I was when married Shiro Morimoto. I knew he be killed in South Sea, and if so I never have second husband. Japanese boy marry only virgin girl. Then I find you and love you, but I know deep in my heart someday you leave Hanako and go back to America and marry American girl. I not cry, I promise.'

As she spoke she opened the door to the little wooden cage, picked up the grasshopper, and poised it on the tip of her finger. As if echoing her words – its song ceased.

Upon his arrival at the Press Club Joe found a letter awaiting him from the editor of his paper. He opened it, expecting the usual list of instructions and story suggestions submitted to him every Monday, and was shocked, dumbfounded to find, instead, an urgent notice recalling him to the States 'on a matter which I shall discuss with you privately in my office'.

So they had found out about Hanako! They wanted him home either to fire him, or to shut him up in the Los Angeles office to write the obituaries.

Well, he was not going to submit to their blackmail. He was not going to leave Hanako or Japan. He would send in his resignation and get a job teaching in one of the colleges. After venting his fury and disgust with three double Scotches, it was almost with relief that he went to the library to compose his reply.

Scott Greenway was sitting at a desk bent over a Japanese book. He looked up, said: 'Hello, son. What's new?'

'Plenty!' Joe exploded. 'I've been recalled to the States. Probably to be sacked.'

Scott said sadly: 'Hanako?'

'God damned to hell, I don't know!'

'What are you going to do?'

'Resign. What else?'

'Don't.'

'If you think I'm going back to the States and leave Hanako . . . '

'Take her with you.'

Joe sat down with a thump. Such a thought had never occurred to him. In the first place she had refused to marry him. In the second place he didn't want to leave Japan. In the third place no Japanese national was permitted to leave the country.

'But that's impossible! I've asked her to marry me, and she refused.'

'Possibly because you never mentioned taking her to America. There are many reasons why a Japanese girl can't marry a foreigner and live in Japan at the present time. Perhaps in two years – five . . . '

'I know. She drew me a pretty good map. But even if Hanako agreed to come she couldn't get an exit permit.'

'She might.'

'And in America . . . ' He stopped short, blushing to the roots of his hair.

Scott said quietly: 'That's your problem. And it is a problem – a serious one. You shouldn't be embarrassed to admit it. We must all face up to it.' He brushed aside the book he was reading and looked straight into Joe's eyes.

In a formal, distant way they had become good friends. They had often talked about immaterial things, but had never got around to fundamentals, never finished a serious conversation that was started. Scott had listened to Joe, but had never counselled him, though ever since they had first met he seemed to know intuitively what was in the back of Joe's mind, what was troubling him, sometimes appearing to want to share a deep personal confidence with him, yet never quite coming to the point.

'Son,' he said, 'you and I have discovered something I don't think the other lads here have. I mean in this country.' Joe nodded, and Scott went on: 'Maybe others don't look at things the same way, but I think we've found – it's difficult to put into words – a certain way of life. I won't let it go easily, and I don't think you will either.'

Joe remained silent. Scott continued: 'You and I will come back to Japan one day. I'm sure of it. But this is not the right time. Things are too close, too raw, too one-sided. There are too many restrictions for the Japanese – for Hanako-san – for Midori-san.'

'Midori-san?'

'My wife.'

'Your wife!'

'You met her once here at the club – in the bar. We were married three days ago. She's a Japanese lady, well known in Tokyo, and teaches flower arrangement. She's written many books on the subject. In fact, I was just glancing over this latest one now.'

'But how did you get permission to marry – if you're not resigning from your job?'

'You don't need permission, Joe. No one can stop you from marrying who you wish. It's what happens after they find out. GHQ can cancel your passport, so you can't live in Japan, or the Japanese can refuse your wife an exit visa. I've been lucky. I happen to be on good terms with the colonel and he has given Midori a permit to leave with me in a week's time.'

'You're leaving!' Suddenly Joe felt sad and confused. If Scott was leaving, and he could not marry Hanako, there was not much left for him in Japan. On the other hand, if Scott could get a visa for his wife – if Joe could persuade Hanako to marry him and leave Japan . . .

As if reading his mind, Scott said shortly: 'I'm sorry, Joe. I can't squeeze the lemon twice. However, there is one possible solution. I might be able to persuade the colonel that it's necessary for Midori to bring her personal maid with her to the States.'

'God, Scott! If you could do that . . .'

'Hanako could accompany us to the plane at Tachikawa Air Base, and you could show up at the last minute. Then you're on your own. We'll only be in the States for one month. I've been transferred to the London office.'

'I'll miss you, Scott. I don't know what Hanako will say about all this, but . . .'

'Get tough with her. These girls can take it. If she loves you, that is.'

'I'll try. God, I'll try!'

'And, Joe — I don't know how you'll make out with your chief back home. If you do get Hanako to the States it might not be easy for either of you. If it gets too tough you might try London — they're used to mixed marriages — the Commonwealth, you know. Anyway, think it over. It would be nice to meet up with you again.'

'Thanks, Scott. Thanks for everything,' Joe said.

They lay together on the bed roll in Hanako's little hill-top house watching the moon through the open *shoji*.

'No, Joe-san,' she said. 'I have told you — it is not possible. Even in America. I have bad marriage, you have bad marriage. What make you think our marriage be better? Hanako never marry again! Never!'

'Listen to me,' he pleaded. 'There's no other way. We love each other. It must work out! It will!'

'How you know it will?'

'Because once we're married we can face up to anything — anybody. Nothing can touch us. There'll be just you and me.'

'Just you and me?'

'I received a letter from the editor of my paper today. I've been recalled to Los Angeles. This is our last chance for happiness. Don't you understand? I must leave Japan within three days. With or without you!'

He could feel her stiffen, feel the trembling of her fingers against his cheek.

'You leave Japan? So soon?'

'I must. I told you we can't go on living together like this for ever – as generous as you have been with your love.'

She said in a whisper: 'I not know what to do, Joe-san. I think I cannot live without you, without your touch upon my body, but people will treat Hanako very bad, just as in Japan.'

'Of course they won't! They'll love you as much as I do. Believe me. Trust me.'

After a long pause, she said: 'Just you and Hanako? No other people? No other thing?'

'Just you and I.'

'Promise?'

'Promise.'

'I think about it, *anata*. We make love now by light of moon, and when first light of day touch *shoji*, I give answer, yes?'

Chapter Eleven

They were married at the Shinto shrine on the hill-top over-looking Kamakura. It was a simple, very beautiful ceremony presided over by the priest in a white silken robe with winged sleeves topped by a tall black cone-shaped hat. Hanako and Joe stood side by side beneath the low thatched roof under the cluster of straw ropes and strips of rice paper while the priest read from a Japanese scroll, chanting in a high-pitched voice as he waved a feather wand over their heads to cleanse their sins.

Hanako looked lovely in her red and gold kimono with one long sleeve hanging down to the floor and her *obi* raised to the nape of the neck for the sacred occasion. It all made little sense to Joe, but obviously Hanako was deeply affected. No longer was there any trace of tension, fear, or doubt on her face. She stood by his side straight and proud, her black eyes shining out like fires from her golden face.

Only when the priest had stopped chanting and offered them two tiny cups of cold *sake* which he took from the altar did she show any emotion. A single tear fell upon her cheek as she drank from the cup, her head bowed. Joe, watching her, felt then the sorrow and the heartbreak that he knew weighed upon her and that she must bear for the rest of her life – the loss of her daughter Naoko.

But she said not a word, and when the ceremony was over, took his arm and walked down the winding pathway to her house where she would change and take leave of Joe before joining Scott Greenway and his wife at their Tokyo hotel.

She had made up her mind and there was no turning back. She had married a foreigner because she loved him, but she would never be able to return to Japan – that she knew and accepted. She had registered their marriage with the authorities, had obtained her exit permit after her family record and her moral behaviour had been checked by the police, and now she would spend twenty-four hours in Tokyo with the Greenways before joining Joe at the air base where they would take off for Guam, Hawaii, and Los Angeles – her new home – her new life.

She must not think of Naoko, or ever speak of the pain in her breast. It was not for a Japanese girl to complain, to regret. She loved Joe, and in spite of the fact that only a short time ago she had been considered an enemy by the Americans, an American had asked her for her hand, and she had accepted him. Japan – the terrible war years – the dreadful poverty – her unhappy marriage and the humiliation she had suffered under her father-in-law's roof – the insults heaped upon her by her compatriots – were all behind her. She was about to set off on a new path, live in a new world bright with promise. Already she looked back upon Japan with bitterness and resentment, with a hardening of her heart. But it was all in the past, and with Joe to lead her and shield her, together they would fly to America, the most hospitable, the most generous, the most affluent country in the world to live out their lives in happiness and peace.

The giant C54 Army Air Force Transport plane stood on the apron, its engines coughing. The Greenways, along with several other reporters and servicemen on leave, had already taken their seats, while Hanako waited at the foot of the steps anxiously searching the highway that led to the base for sight of Joe.

The minutes passed and he did not come. Perspiration dampened her dress and ran down her forehead as she stood in the hot sunshine wondering what would become of her if something should have gone wrong, if the plane took off without him. The revving of the engines told her the pilot would not wait long. Should she join the Greenways, take a chance that if Joe missed the plane, he would follow on the next one? Or should she simply run out of the gate and return to Kamakura and forget that she had ever met him?

Why was he late? He must know how she felt! She would never forgive him!

A cloud of dust was visible on the highway. Her heart leaped. She saw it was a jeep driven by a soldier, but she could not see the passenger. It was approaching the gate, going very fast, skidding all over the road. Behind the jeep was another car – she recognized it at once – a Japanese police car, its siren wailing. Was Joe in trouble? She saw him now, leaning forward, waving! She ran towards the gate just as the jeep drew up with screaming brakes in front of the sentries.

And then, with a gasp of disbelief, she saw her! Her daughter Naoko! Joe was holding her in his arms, wrapped in a blanket.

He was talking to an MP, waving his pass. And then he jumped from the jeep and ran to her, ran into her arms, and together they crossed the apron, climbed the steps, and boarded the plane.

The door shut behind them. As Hanako hugged her daughter to her breast, out of the window they saw the policeman, surrounded by MPs, furiously waving his arms.

PART TWO

1965

Japanese girls are not used to husbands they can order
around. The shock of their being able to do so can
undermine their whole system and state of mind.

Scott Greenway

Chapter Twelve

Mother and daughter pushed their way through the swinging doors of Swan and Edgar's in Piccadilly Circus smiling happily over their purchases at the June sale.

'I was terribly afraid I couldn't afford my handbag,' Naoko said delightedly. 'It took all my week's allowance. Anyway, I won't have to ask Daddy for a loan.'

'I should think not!' Hanako admonished her. 'Your father has been far too generous as it is. Now we must hurry and catch bus or I'll be late to prepare dinner.'

They turned the corner and walked down Piccadilly, intending to cross the street to the bus-stop opposite Simpson's, when they were confronted with two large coaches which had drawn up in front of the hotel to unload their passengers. To Naoko's surprise the tourists were all Japanese. She stared curiously, almost longingly, at them as they disembarked and gathered in groups on the kerb dressed in tight-fitting business suits, clutching cameras and jabbering to one another in shrill, high-pitched voices.

One elderly man holding up a wallet talked excitedly to the doorman, who stared at him with open mouth, unable to comprehend a word he said. Finally, in desperation, the Japanese spoke to the bus-driver, who also shrugged him off. It was then that he noted Naoko standing in the street smiling at him. He rushed up to her, bowed, and shrilled: *'Ojo-san, chotto, chotto, tasukete kudasaimasen ka? Hikoki no kippu o nusumareta-n-desuyo. Ko-no-hito ni so itte kuremasen ka?'*

Naoko turned breathlessly to her mother.

'Mummy, what is he saying? What does he want?'

Hanako took her arm, said: 'Come, darling, it is none of our business,' and pulled her away.

'But the man needs help!' Naoko protested. 'Maybe a

thief has stolen his money! Why won't you speak to him?'

'I've told you. We shall be late for dinner,' Hanako replied, and propelled her across the street.

On the bus Naoko sat sulking in silence. She was very angry with her mother for being so rude to the old man who obviously was in need of help. Because of the currency restrictions in Japan, she had met few Japanese, and spoken to none, with the exception of 'Auntie' Greenway who only spoke English at Hanako's request when she came to the house, and her class-mate Miharu, daughter of the Japanese Ambassador. Naoko was curious about her countrymen and eager to meet them, but whenever the occasion had arisen, whether in America or in England, her mother had always managed to evade a confron-tation, as she had today. The fact that she couldn't speak Japanese annoyed Naoko, leaving her with a feeling of embar-rassment and frustration. As a child she had thought nothing of it, had accepted her mother's explanation that, as an American citizen, there was little need to study the language, that to learn the five thousand Kanji and Kana characters would take up all her time and energy when the schools she attended required that she learn English, French, Latin, and Spanish. But now that she was nineteen years old and a sixth-former at St Mary's Hall in Brighton, soon to graduate and forge a life of her own, she blamed her mother for not having encouraged her, indeed, forced her, to at least speak her native tongue.

They got off the bus at Kensington High Street and entered the Mews facing Allen Street which had been their home since leaving the States eight years ago. Hanako opened the door to the ground-floor flat which consisted of a small living room furnished in ultra-modern style, a kitchen and dining alcove filled with the latest electrical appliances purchased at Heal's, two bedrooms, and a small study where Joe often worked long into the night.

Naoko followed her mother into the living room where Joe was seated in his shirtsleeves before the TV listening to the six o'clock news. He got up as they entered, prepared to greet Hanako and kiss his step-daughter, only to have her fling her-self down upon the sofa and burst into tears.

Joe looked at his wife, eyebrows raised.

'What's all this about?' he asked.

Hanako put her parcels on the table and said with a sigh: 'She's just being difficult. She's tired after our little shopping spree. These sales are exhausting.'

'I'm not tired!' Naoko sobbed. 'Why do you have to lie to Daddy? Why don't you tell him the truth!'

'Now, Naoko,' Joe said sternly. 'You mustn't talk to your mother like that.'

'If she won't tell you, then I will! We ran into some Japanese tourists outside the Piccadilly Hotel. One old man was holding up his wallet and trying to make the doorman understand what he was saying. Then he saw us and asked me to help – but I couldn't understand, so I asked Mummy to translate for me. She wouldn't! She dragged me away to catch the bus. She was so rude! Why, Daddy? Why won't she speak to Japanese people? She never will. She treats them like lepers! *Why* – when she's Japanese herself?'

Joe switched off the TV and crossed to her side. He always found it difficult to confront Naoko because, in many ways, she was so much like her mother. She had Hanako's face, her father's height, a premature bustiness, and a resolution to be independent which he recognized only too well. When she was upset, as she was at this moment, her eyes were cat's eyes, like her mother's, wide and slanting. But there was also the charm, the sweetness, the child-like wonder that melted his heart and which had caused him to spoil her as he had Hanako over the years.'

'It's a long story, Naoko,' he said. 'I suppose your mother resents the way your grandfather treated her in Japan after the war – the way so many people treated girls who went out with foreigners at that time.'

'But that was nineteen years ago! The war's over and forgotten! She won't allow a Japanese in the house! Not even Miharu, my own classmate! If we want to meet during vacation, I have to go to *her* house!'

Hanako said: 'Dear, I really don't think it prudent to invite the daughter of the Ambassador here, do you? I'm sure she wouldn't be permitted to come.'

'I'll prove it to you! I'll prove it right now!' She jumped up, crossed to the phone, and started to dial the number.

Hanako stepped forward, snatched the phone from her grasp, and slapped her across the face.

The two stood glaring at one another; then Naoko turned and fled to her room, slamming the door behind her.

'I'm sorry if she upsets you,' Hanako said. 'She can be very naughty at times. I only hope her behaviour – I only hope you don't regret having adopted my obstinate child.'

'Now don't start that again,' Joe said. 'Every time there's a scene you blame Naoko – accuse me of not wanting her here.'

'I not accuse. I blame myself for all the trouble I've caused you – the terrible expense . . .'

'Let me worry about that. I've never complained, have I? And who was it that insisted she have the best education possible?'

'Of course I want her to have the best we can afford. I'm only saying . . .'

'You're saying I shouldn't have kidnapped her in the first place. Is that it?'

'No, no! You've been wonderful, Joe. It's just . . . ' She picked up her parcels, said: 'I'm sorry. Please let's forget,' and started out of the room.

Joe gripped her by the arm. 'No, you don't. We're going to have a talk. We haven't talked for years. Sit down.'

She did as she was told. He lit a cigarette. 'This sort of thing – this infernal bickering – must stop. Let's get it straight. We met – we fell in love – we married. I love you as much as I ever did. We've had bad times, but they're behind us. What's wrong, Hanako? Why this barrier, not only between you and the Japanese, but with Naoko – with me – with everyone!'

'Not you,' she said, tears coming to her eyes. 'Never you, Joe.'

'I don't know what's got into you. You won't speak your language, not even to me. You used to call me *anata*, or Joe-*san*, now it's only Joe, if that. You dislike having friends to the flat, even Scott because he's married to Midori. You won't even cook us a Japanese meal! When I married you you were part of the Japan I'd come to love – a symbol of the Shinto shrines, the crazy *kokeshi* dolls, the little wooden houses with their paper doors and clean white mats, but now – look at this room! This ridiculous furniture! We might be living in an office on top of the Empire State Building!'

'You blame me, I know,' she wept. 'But it's true – I hate Japan and everything to do with it. Why shouldn't I? I had no home, no family, no friends. And then I met you. Now I have a home – our home – and I want to keep it that way – just for you and me. You promised it would be like that. Just the two of us. You promised!'

'Of course I promised. But I never dreamed ...'

'If we're only left alone ...'

'You *can't* shut out the world, Hanako. No matter what I said. You tried that in America and you know what happened.'

'It wasn't entirely my fault, was it? You asked me to marry you, you made me a promise, and you brought me to America. I didn't know then I would be treated like filth as I was in Japan.'

'You weren't treated like filth. There were some bloody awful incidents when we first arrived, but then you went underground. You buried your head in the sand. You made things so difficult I couldn't hold down a job. If Scott hadn't written that there was a vacant spot in *Time-Life*'s subsidiary editing the stupid cook books I don't know what would have become of us. Cook books! The crowning glory for a former foreign correspondent and a budding poet!'

'You don't have to keep job with cook books. You can find other job – you very brilliant man!'

'I agree,' he said sarcastically, hurting her, knowing he was hurting her, wanting to hurt her after all these years of never speaking his mind, of concealing his thoughts and innermost feelings and giving way to her fears and weaknesses until he had become weak and indefensible himself. 'I agree, I am brilliant – a genius! After all, I was offered a job as roving correspondent for the *Reader's Digest*. But what happened? You were afraid to be left alone for a single night. So here I am shut up

101

in this damn prison telling young housewives how to fry an egg!'

He looked up, saw that she was no longer weeping, saw that she was utterly broken, beyond tears, speechless, as he remembered she had behaved under similar circumstances in Japan. Perhaps because of this memory, because it brought back to him a fleeting vision of the wonder and happiness of their courting days when instead of tears there was the light of a thousand mornings in her eyes, instead of her present tight knot of dark hair stranded with grey it fell in a cloud to her shoulders, seeming always to float on currents of light – perhaps because of this vision he crossed to her and, again in a moment of weakness, pity, and love, took her in his arms and kissed her, glad of the touch of her hand on his cheek, grateful for her whispered voice in his ears: 'Oh, Joe-san, *anata*. I love you so much!'

Later, he woke in the night and asked himself what was to become of them. Hanako was curled, as always, in his arms, her incredibly smooth body pressed against his body, her legs intertwined with his, her hair flowing loosely about her bare breasts.

It was during such times, when she was close and asleep by his side, that his love for her was deep and strong, when he put aside their differences, and did not want to hurt her to pursue his interests, even though those interests were as vital to her as to himself. After his lonely childhood and the fiasco of his marriage to Caroline, her warmth and tenderness and grace had become a need so great it overcame any material factor in his life. Though she had rejected her own people and her own language, had spent years in mastering English so that she spoke it practically without a flaw, she still retained the characteristics of the Japanese girl so dear to him; her respect and consideration of him, her rigid code of morality, and her destiny, the result of the perfection of her training, to assure his happiness and well being. She still asked his permission to leave their bed in the morning before setting about the day's chores: cooking breakfast, washing the personal linen, fitting new covers to the living-room furniture, making a new curtain or a new dress which she always designed and cut herself. She also did the shopping, having long ago conquered the nausea of preparing such alien Western delicacies as grilled kidneys, lambs' hearts, calves' brains, sweetbreads, tripe, stewed oxtail, prunes and junket.

And yet in spite of this, in spite of the fact that he had at last been able to share his heart with another human being, something was lacking in their marriage. Perhaps it was just because her love for him was so disciplined, so generous and dependable, because she had tried so hard to make an earthly Paradise for them in the face of their past and present difficulties, that he felt restricted, smothered by her love. Real love was a gift, not a possession. He realized it was a sad paradox in that he would have given his life for such devotion in his marriage to Caroline, nevertheless it was a fact, as it was a fact that he felt somehow cheated. He had married a girl whom he thought loved Japan, as he did, yet who would not return even for a visit – a girl who was Japanese, yet who, outside their bedroom, had done all she could to conceal it from the world. Had he not found out in the nick of time that she had made an appointment with a doctor to have her upper eyelids slashed to make the Mongolian fold fall back into place enabling her to lose her Japanese look completely?

Something had to be done – they couldn't go on drifting for ever. There had been moments in the past when, faced with an appalling situation, he had feared for her sanity. There was the time when a prospective employer had told him face to face that he would not risk hiring Joe because his wife was Japanese – not that she wasn't a lady or because she was a former enemy of the Americans, but because of the gossip and the innuendoes that would arise and which was bound to affect Joe's work. And there was the party he gave for her at a friend's house upon their arrival in Los Angeles. He had invited the editor of his newspaper in the hopes that he would like Hanako and not fire him as seemed likely from the tone of the telegram he had received in Tokyo.

His friend had invited two hundred guests and hired a maid

103

to help out. The guests started to arrive, but there was no sign of Hanako.

Through the window Joe could see the traffic pulling up on the street before the front door. Brakes screamed and people shouted. Finally Joe ran out to see what was the matter. There he found Hanako in a kimono receiving the guests on the pavement, bowing, in Japanese tradition, four times to each new arrival before escorting them into the house and presenting them to the bewildered maid.

Joe lost his job, and Hanako never wore a kimono again.

He could look back on it now with a certain amount of amusement, as he did when they were bathing at the Biltmore Casino in Santa Barbara while visiting his mother. Joe went to change in the men's room, neglecting to inform Hanako that the Santa Barbarans – providentially perhaps – clothed their bodies in swimsuits. When he emerged and met her beside the crowded pool, he was more than a little startled to discover her stark as the day she was born.

But there had been other incidents not so amusing, such as when they were refused a hotel room in New Orleans because they considered her 'black'. And more recently, when she was elbowed out of a queue on Kensington High Street because 'I'm not having a Jap served before me'.

These indignities, eighteen years after the war, were deeply distressing to Hanako, and were the fundamental cause of her emotionally disturbed state of mind. The wives of the other Japanese residents living in London apparently faced the same indignities, but somehow managed to surmount them, possibly because they mixed with one another, shared their experiences as well as the means to combat them. Not so Hanako. She stood out as a solitary figure of a girl in a strange and indifferent country whose only reason for existing was her love for Joe and the care of their home, of which her own daughter Naoko remained a bright if incidental supplement.

Chapter Thirteen

They sat in the booth at the George and Dragon across the street from the *Time-Life* Building where they met once a week over a Guinness. Scott had not changed much. Had his hair not turned chalk white, he might have been taken for forty, not sixty. His body remained firm, his stomach flat. He was still composed, gentle, unpretentious in spite of the fact that now he was chief of *Time*'s London Bureau as well as the author of many successful novels, the outcome, no doubt, of his continued sense of youth and his unceasing interest and zest for life.

'Well, how's the famous gastronomist?' he grinned. 'You must be a first-class cook by now. Have you taken over from Hanako?' He saw the look of pain in Joe's eyes, said: 'Sorry, but you didn't have to take the job.'

'I know. Don't get me wrong. I'm grateful to you, Scott — for so many things.'

'Rot. If you want to go back to reporting I guess it can be arranged.'

'Forget it. You know Hanako . . .'

'I thought I did.'

Joe frowned. 'Is it so obvious? I know how stupid she's being about the Japanese, but I hope you don't take it personally — you and Midori.'

'Of course not. Hanako needs a good spanking to make her snap out of herself. She can join the Japanese Women's Association, the *Otomodachi-kai*, attend the lunches at the Nippon Club. Midori is a member of them all and would see that she took part in the activities and met the Embassy wives.'

'But she won't. You know she won't.'

'Right. I don't want to get involved in your personal affairs, Joe, but you've been too weak with her. Japanese girls are not used to husbands they can order around. The shock of Hanako being able to do so has obviously undermined her whole system and state of mind.'

'It isn't that, Scott. I'm still the boss. It's just I haven't wanted to get tough with her – we've been through quite a lot in the States and – well, I tried getting tough once and it almost ended in tragedy. That was when I wrote to you from New York and you saved my life by setting us up over here.' He took a long draught of beer. 'I suppose I have been weak with her, but I didn't want to lose her – in more ways than one. Now it's too late – it's all a mess.'

Scott was silent for a time, lost in thought. Then he turned and looked Joe squarely in the eye.

'Why haven't you and Hanako had any kids?'

'Don't ask me. We never use any preventatives – not that I'm aware of, anyway. Hanako simply says: "If it happens, it happens," but she's damned secretive about it. I don't think she really wants a child. She keeps a weird collection of herbs locked up in her dresser drawer and it could just be she puts them in her tea or something. I wouldn't know. She said once that she couldn't have a child because she visited Hiroshima a week after it was bombed and it affected her in some way. I think it's a lot of bullshit. She still thinks a child of mixed blood will get the same treatment here as he does in Japan.'

'Surely there must be some way you can trick her into it. Slip a micky in her martini. Surprise her when she's asleep.'

'She doesn't drink martinis,' Joe said ruefully. 'And I wouldn't fool her like that. If she doesn't want a kid, there'd be all hell to pay if she had one. She's emotionally disturbed enough, as it is.'

Scott lit a cigarette. After a long silence he said: 'Joe, I want you to do something for me. In fact, it's an order. It's been on my mind for weeks, and yesterday we had a meeting and reached a decision.'

'About what?'

'As you know, we've covered most of the European countries, North and South America, and the next cook book should be on Japanese food. One hundred appetising recipes – *sukiyaki, domburi, tempura, sashimi*. Also a section on Japanese table manners – preparation of teas and wines – rice sandwiches – festival dishes – the lot.'

106

'You mean . . . ?'

'Exactly. Who else is better suited for the job? You're not only an expert on the culinary art, but you know Japan. Take Hanako with you. She could be of help. All expenses paid.'

Joe's eyes gleamed. The mere thought of returning to Japan sent his heart beating wildly. The depression which had gripped him over the last years, the prostration of body and soul, suddenly lifted. Scott's offer seemed to come as an answer to all his troubles.

'I can't think of any assignment I'd like better! But will Hanako go?'

'Make her. I told you once before to get tough with her. You did and she behaved like a lamb.'

'Why are you giving *me* this chance? In Tokyo you said you'd go back to Japan one day – that you'd found a certain way of life . . . '

'I will. When I retire. We've bought a little hideaway in Chiba – Midori's mother is living there now – keeping it warm for us.'

'It would be a wonderful thing for us both if Hanako would go back. She'd have to tear down this barrier she's erected for no reason. It's just something she's built up in her mind as a sort of protection against being hurt . . . '

'Then it's settled.' Scott smiled, drained his glass, and stood up. 'I'll call the Japanese Air Lines and book seats for the two of you a week from today. Okay?'

'Okay,' Joe said softly. 'This time *I'm* going to call the tune.' As they walked together to the door, he suddenly tapped Scott on the shoulder. 'You're sure this isn't another of your life-saving gestures? I bet you a dollar you never held a meeting yesterday. I bet you just thought it up on the spur of the moment.'

'Could be,' Scott laughed. 'But if we haven't held a meeting, we'll hold one now. So start packing.'

Joe didn't mention his plans until they had finished dinner, and yet his excitement must have been evident, for Hanako was unusually silent during the meal, her mind and body braced, as it were, for a scene she intuitively felt was forthcoming.

He questioned Naoko about her 'A' Level examinations which she had taken two weeks before, and though she would not have the results until September, she assured him with her customary aplomb that she had passed them all. In the back of his mind he was already making arrangements for her to spend the summer in Italy so that they would not be burdened with her. It was vitally important that he and Hanako went alone on this assignment so that they could recapture the past and build upon it a future without fear or prejudice, a solid basis for a new life.

When Naoko had washed up in the kitchen and retired to her room, and Hanako had settled down in front of the TV, Joe said: 'Don't switch it on. I have something important to tell you.'

She stiffened. 'Please, Joe, not tonight. I'm very tired and I must look after Naoko's packing. Her half-term's up to-morrow.'

'Yes, I know. But this won't take long. In fact, it can be said in five words: "We're going back to Japan".'

If he thought she would scream, or faint, or laugh in his face, he was disappointed. She said softly: 'I not go to Japan, Joe, ever again. It would hurt me if you go because I love you with all my heart. You take job in Tokyo?'

'The office is sending me – *us* – on a three months' assignment – all expenses paid. We leave next week. The seats are booked.'

'I'll miss you, Joe. How I shall live without you I don't know. How will my body sleep without your body close to me at night? But I must let you go because Hanako has been too selfish in the past. I know this now – how unhappy I've made you – how you lose many jobs because of me – how angry you speak to me in America so I try *hara-kiri* not to hurt you any more – so you could forget Hanako and marry American girl . . .'

'Damn it, Hanako, shut up! That's all forgotten. Listen to me. We're going to Japan. I'm ordering you to come! You understand?'

She got to her feet, crossed to him, and took his head in her hands, touching his lips and eyes and face with a caress so tender and with such boundless warmth that it took all his courage not to sweep her into his arms and tell her he would not leave her, could never leave her, that he would tell Scott Greenway to go to hell.

He knew, then, that she would not go with him to Japan, and that he could not force her to do so. After nineteen years of marriage he had lost the power to use force, to ill treat her, belittle her, or order her around as perhaps he should. He had too much respect for her, his love for her was too great, too all-engulfing to hurt her mentally or physically, and yet he was very angry with her, and himself, and in his anger and frustration he was determined to accept the assignment – possibly his last opporunity to ever see Japan again – even if it meant going alone. There was the danger that, in her unhappiness, she might again do something silly, attempt suicide, but he could not live his life under a constant threat. For her sake, as well as his own, he must risk her blackmail, clothed, as it was, in declarations of devotion, in the sincere hope that it was only a threat, a threat which, once challenged, would prove unwarranted and ineffectual.

They were interrupted by the entrance of Naoko, her arms full of clothing that she was about to pack. In his anger and bitterness, Joe swung round to her, and with his back to Hanako, said: 'Naoko – how would you like to visit the country of your birth?'

They sat together in the first-class compartment of JAL's DC 8 peering down at the great citadels of ice, towers, and castles that was the high Arctic. Though they could not make out much of the landscaping or see any trace of the reindeer, polar bears, penguins, Dall sheep, musk oxen, lemmings, shrews, moles, and field mice which the captain explained over the loudspeaker lived, bred, fought, ate, spawned, and died there beneath the snow, Naoko was fascinated by the flight, having, in her usual thorough fashion, read up on every aspect of the trip, detailing for Joe the early explorations of the Arctic and the pioneers who had made the Polar Flight possible: John Cabot, in the service of England; Martin Frobisher, one of Good Queen Bess' 'sea dogs'; William Baffin, Vitus Bering, Fritjof Nansen, Roald Amundsen, Commodore Peary, Lincoln Ellsworth, Floyd Bennet, and Admiral Byrd. She also enlightened him about the instruments used by the navigator on the flight deck: the 'weather eye' radar which gave warning of an approaching storm, and the Bendix Polar Path gyroscope which they needed when the compass was out of action, as it was twice a year during the Arctic twilight when the sun was below the horizon.

Listening to her, watching her out of the corner of his eye, he was struck dumb by her knowledge – rather the intensity of her interest, her eagerness to learn, to see, to explore, to question, and as he listened, nodding his approval, he realized, with a pang of regret, how little he knew his step-daughter, what she felt about Japan, America, England – how she felt about him. When she was not in boarding school, where she was most of the year, she was visiting her classmates in Sussex or Kent, picking hops, riding horseback, swimming in the sea. He did not even know that she could swim until he had found her packing her suit one morning. How did she learn? Where did she learn? And to ride? She had even won a blue ribbon for show-jumping!

It was his fault, of course. Or was it? He had his job to do – and deep down he supposed he had been as relieved as Hanako to have her off their hands so that their life would not be disturbed any more than it was already. And, of course, Hanako's one thought had always been to shut out the world, to exclude everyone from their home, even her own daughter. Sitting beside her now, her arm in his, he felt it was a miracle Naoko cared for him enough to leave her school and her friends in mid-term to fly away alone with a man she called Daddy, yet scarcely knew, a man whom she must have felt had neglected her and treated her abominably.

As they approached Anchorage lying at the foot of the snow-capped Chugach mountains, Joe fastened his seat belt and sat back enjoying the sight of the Japanese air hostesses in their blue and white kimonos distributing their hot, cologne-scented towels on slippered feet, so *petite*, attentive, and gracious compared with the Western hostesses he had rubbed up against with their rasping, nasal voices and instant smiles who offered assorted sweets to their charges as if they were delinquent children. For Joe the scene was a happy one, a welcome forecast of what was to come, a small glimpse of the Japan that he remembered with fondness akin to love.

Not until they had left Anchorage to the blaring tune of 'Squaws Along the Yukon', and swung out over the ink-dark waters of the Pacific on their way to Tokyo's International Airport, did Naoko turn to him and ask:

'Why didn't Mummy come with us?'

'I've told you. She's got a bug about Japan.'

She was silent, looking out of the window. 'Is Mummy ill, Daddy?'

'Ill? Of course not. Why do you ask?'

'She acts so strange at times. I can't explain it exactly – I thought you might be able to.'

After a moment, when he told himself that they would be together for three months and must be honest with each other, he said: 'I think perhaps she is, Naoko.'

'How, Daddy? Why?'

'I don't know. Your grandfather once said that a person could be spiritually misplaced. I took no notice of him at the time, but now I wonder if perhaps he was right. Actually it's a sort of never-ending nervous breakdown. Why? It's hard to say. When we were married your mother expected everything to be perfect – I did too, I suppose. And it wasn't. We were both trying to escape from our pasts and didn't face the realities of the present. We never thought beyond the bedroom. Hanako has a guilt complex because she feels she has lost me some important jobs. That's true, but it was my fault as much as hers because I wasn't firm enough with her from the beginning. I couldn't bring myself to bully her because I could see the stress she was under – how she reacted to the stupid indignities and cruelties heaped upon her when we arrived in the States.'

'Was it really that bad, Daddy?'

'It doesn't seem so now – it's water down the drain, but at the time your mother wasn't prepared for it and she's never got over the shock.'

'I don't remember.'

'No, you wouldn't. You were only a kid and we kept you in school as much as possible.'

'Tell me about it.'

'I don't know that I should. What good would it do?'

'Maybe it will help me to understand her. Maybe you should have told me long ago.'

'Maybe I should,' he said, and was silent in thought. He took a deep breath. 'There were many incidents – too many to detail, but all more or less alike. We were refused rooms in hotels – membership to clubs. I was fired from my newspaper job because I had married a Jap. I found other jobs, but it was always the same. She was treated like a servant – worse, a prostitute. They thought she was game for any white man who wanted her – weren't all Japs? they'd say – and humiliated her in the open streets. We moved from one state to another – it was always the same – worse in the South where they called her "High Yeller".

'It was there she had her first real fright. A big buck Negro grabbed her one night on her way home from a movie. I was working night shift at a lumberyard in Columbia. He dragged her into a dark alley and tried to rape her. Luckily a policeman appeared just in time and took her away unconscious to hospital. They put her in the coloured ward. You can imagine how she felt when she woke up and found she was surrounded by the same sort of jerks who'd tried to rape her. She started screaming and they had to give her a sedative.

'We moved to Philadelphia, Washington, finally to New York. By this time she wouldn't let me out of her sight. I was desperate for work, but she wouldn't let me take a job. And then one day we were invited to a party given by a pal of mine I'd met at the Tokyo Press Club. He was a newspaper man, but had taken a job with the *Reader's Digest*. I asked him if he could help me out and he said there was an opening for a roving correspondent. Hanako overheard the conversation, broke in, and gave him hell for even suggesting it. I was so angry, so frustrated, I slapped her face and told her in no uncertain terms what I thought of her in front of the guests.

'I didn't know she would take it so hard. Anyway, when we got back from the party she locked herself in the bathroom and cut her wrists.' He sighed. 'So now you know.'

After a long silence Naoko said: 'Poor Mummy.'

PART THREE

1965

We gave the Japanese a bit of sound advice: to give up militarism and concentrate on economics. Unfortunately, they followed our advice.

Dennis Garvan

Chapter Fourteen

They reached the northern tip of Hokkaido and started the long descent to Haneda Airport. Joe recognized the mountains broken by the narrow dirt roads that wound through the forests of cedar and pine to the scattered toy villages with their unpainted wooden shacks and blacktiled roofs, and his heart tightened. Nothing had changed. It was still the same strange, beautiful country that he remembered.

They were met at the foot of the gangway by two smiling representatives of Japan Air Lines who swiftly guided them through Customs and hustled them, along with their luggage, into a waiting chauffeur-driven Toyota Century limousine. He smiled to himself as he took his seat beside Naoko, half expecting to find himself riding in one of the old charcoal-burning Fords which had been the sole means of private transportation after the war and which he had come to associate with the weird know-how of the Japanese people, an association which was quickly dispelled as they turned out of the airport on to a sweeping four-lane expressway that lay on top of the stores and shops which had once been wooden shacks teeming with life. If below them kimono-clad figures still came and went about their business, they were not visible as the car sped past monstrous new skyscrapers, a baseball field, a race track, a sporting arena, a skating rink, overtaken only by the train on the monorail as it slid noiselessly to its destination in the heart of the city.

Peering out of the window, Naoko gasped:

'It's fabulous! More fantastic than New York! I thought you said Japan was a land of wooden houses, paper doors, shrines, and windbells!'

'There do seem to have been a few changes,' Joe grinned. 'That's only to be expected. But Tokyo isn't Japan. You'll see. Give it time.'

117

After fifteen minutes they left the expressway and passed through a built-up area where men, women, and children were working, mending, dismantling. Large lorries loaded to the brim roared along beside them taking no notice whatever of the pedestrians or the spluttering motor-cycles and scooters which cut across their paths with serene disregard. Somewhere in the midst of this bedlam children ran about, vendors pushed their noodle carts, dogs howled, horses neighed, and at the road crossings stalled trams blasted their trumpets, operated by compressed air, like prehistoric beasts gone mad.

They reached the shopping centre of Shimbashi which Joe hardly recognized with its wide streets and gleaming modern office buildings. They passed a television tower higher than the Eiffel Tower rising grotesquely above Shiba Park, but farther on, to Joe's immense relief, a beautiful golden temple stood sedately in its immaculate garden, its three gabled roofs facing the sky like upturned gilded umbrellas.

He proudly pointed it out to Naoko, who gasped at its beauty. 'You see,' he said emotionally, 'Japan is small, crowded, sometimes vulgarly modern, yet here in the centre of the capital you come face to face with its true spirit – one of its ancient shrines.' He tapped the chauffeur on the shoulder. 'Would you mind – could you stop here for a few minutes? We'd like to see the shrine.'

The Japanese driver giggled, then clapped his hand over his mouth.

'Not mind, sir. But so sorry – that new Chinese restaurant. Holds three thousand people every night – has best calypso orchestra in Tokyo.'

Joe and Naoko looked at one another. Naoko burst out laughing. Joe, struggling to hide his chagrin, said ruefully: 'You fooled me that time,' then remained silent until they reached the hotel.

The Imperial Hotel, with its yellow brick façade and lily pond facing the moat and the Imperial Palace, appeared to Joe to be the only building he recognized in Tokyo. Though he understood it was to be torn down in a year's time to be replaced by a modern one, it was with a feeling of nostalgia that he followed the bellboy to the suite on the second floor consisting of two bedrooms separated by a luxurious bathroom.

He felt exhausted after the long flight, and when he had unpacked and bathed he knocked on Naoko's door.

'Tired? Want to take a nap?' he asked.

'Are you joking? I want to see Tokyo. Every mile of it – tonight!'

'That's a tall order. You could spend a whole day just wandering through the arcade downstairs.'

'What time is it?' she asked, slipping off her blouse and turning on the bath water.

'Just after six.'

'You have a nap. I'll wake you in an hour. You're taking me to a Japanese restaurant, and then to a nightclub. I hear they're fab – and very sexy!'

'What do you know about sex?' he smiled, a disapproving eye on her bulging bra and bare torso.

'Oh, enough to get along.'

He was shocked, in spite of himself, and once again struck by the fact that he knew little about her, and nothing whatever about her morals. But then he supposed young girls did become women almost overnight.

'You mean you aren't a virgin?' he asked severely, aware as he did so of his astonishment as well as his inability to cope with a situation obviously outside his authority, at least in her eyes.

'Daddy! You should know better than that! Ask me no questions and I'll tell you no lies.'

'Oh,' he said, flustered. 'Well, perhaps you're right. But this country has a permissive society and if I were you . . . '

'But you aren't me, Daddy.' Then throwing her arms about his neck, she kissed him and laughed: 'Don't worry, I can look after myself. I'm not going to disgrace you, I promise. Now go take your nap while I have my bath.'

He went back and lay on the bed, but, as weary as he was, sleep did not come. He lay looking out of the window at the scaffolding of yet another skyscraper rising next door, watched the ceaseless activity of the little men with their yellow tin hats, the tall yellow cranes, the machinery spotlit by fierce arcs, strangely disturbed by the lingering warmth of Naoko's high, full breasts against his chest which mingled with the image of Hanako. It did not come to haunt him from halfway across the world, but from his memory of her in Japan, in Atami, her body etched against the blue of the sea like a medallion of gold, her hair falling in a wondrous wealth down her back, like Naoko's. Sometimes they looked so much alike – at least in his mind – that he could not tell them apart.

The porter gave them a list of selected restaurants and night-clubs in the neighbourhood, and Joe chose Akahane, combining pleasure with work. Not one restaurant on the list had existed when he was last in Tokyo, and he was amazed by the trans-formation, the imposing bars, coffee houses, theatres, and dance halls with their blazing neon lights that had sprung up like bamboo shoots after a spell of rain. It was all too strange, too incredible for him to digest on this first night in this gargantuan metropolis of pleasure and entertainment, still recalling, as he did, its wide patches of scorched emptiness, streets without names with their forlorn kerbside stalls strung with bare lights on overhead wiring, frequented by women in bloomers and men in rags. For Naoko, walking by his side, her hand in his, it was a fairyland, as it obviously was for the handsome youths who jostled them as they hurried past, all going somewhere with a purpose – an army that never knew the war. For Joe it was bewildering, disappointing, all rather sad. Even the inhabitants seemed to have changed – grown taller, less courteous, no longer concerned about everyday trivial things, blinded by the industrial achievement, the tall buildings that blotted out the sun, the garish forest of neon lights.

At the Akahane they were presented with a spread beyond their wildest dreams. Served on lacquered trays, the hors d'œuvre consisted of thin slices of raw tuna and a basket of baby crabs the size of spiders, which they ate, basket and all, as it was made of seaweed. Fried honey-bees followed, and salted thrush hearts served with rough mountain mushrooms and spidery wild chrysanthemum leaves. Then a mixed grill composed of broiled quail, assorted song birds and woodcock balanced by deep pink and golden yellow slices of sausage made of smoked duck and fresh ginger. The food – a work of art – was endless. Throughout the meal Joe took notes and was assured by the manager that he could return at his convenience to photograph the masterpiece in colour.

Later they went to the Club White Heron on the Ginza. It was a large club lit with paper lanterns. A rising and sinking revolving dais brought the performers within a few feet of their table, which Joe found exciting because the huge cabaret consisted of geisha girls clad in elaborate kimonos. He felt he had been lucky in his choice, as the whole scene and tone of the club was redolent of yesteryears of Tokyo; he was sure that Naoko was impressed.

After the show he asked her to dance, brushing aside the aggressive hostesses who clustered around him not once glancing at Naoko, dismissing her as if she did not exist. Holding her in his arms while they danced, he was glad he had not come back to Japan alone. It was nice having such a charming companion. He told himself that together they would explore, not only Tokyo, but the more primitive islands, such as Hokkaido. He would not need to submit to the embarrassing attentions of Japan's little waxworks robots with Naoko to keep him company.

It was getting on to midnight when they left the club and started walking back to the hotel. They had only gone a few blocks when Naoko stopped in front of an open door brightly lit with advertisements. Pop music poured out of the entrance through loudspeakers. Though Joe couldn't understand the Japanese words, he recognized the song as one of the Beatles'.

'Daddy, let's look in here for a minute.'

'Are you crazy? That's a discothèque. I thought you wanted to see *Japan*. You were always accusing your mother . . . '

'But this is Japan, too, Daddy! You can have your stuffy old geishas. Please!'

He shrugged, realizing with a pang of remorse that she had not really enjoyed the evening so far, or the elaborate cabaret, and following her in silence down the narrow stone stairs to the basement. He had hardly set foot in the crowded room when he was nearly blinded by the strobe lights that flashed on and off in flickering sequence, keeping time, it seemed, to the screaming speakers installed in the white floor.

They were shown to a small table in one corner by a Japanese girl trailing what looked like a bed sheet. At the same moment another girl placed two glasses of Suntory whisky before them, and a dish filled with peanuts. The heat, the music, the noise, the sickly fragrance of smouldering joss-sticks, the blinding lights, all blended together to paralyse Joe's mind. He gulped down his drink and ordered another.

He was the only Occidental in the room, and the only male over twenty. As he looked about him at the Japanese youths 'doing their thing', dancing or petting or lying sprawled out on the benches in their jeans and chequered shirts eyeing him with arrogant disdain, he remembered how, during his last visit to Japan, such insolent behaviour would have resulted in their being beaten or locked up. A gathering such as this of more than three males in one room or even on a street corner would have been fair game for the MPs. He had always felt guilty and ashamed when the Japanese were pushed around by the Occupation Forces, but now he was not sure how he felt about it, or if it had not been a good thing after all.

He sighed. Maybe he was getting old!

A Japanese youth, naked to the waist, wearing tight-fitting velvet trousers, approached the table and spoke to Naoko, completely ignoring Joe. Though she could not understand him, it was obvious he was asking her to dance, and without a word she stood up and followed him on to the floor. Joe watched them as they joined the crowd, drowning his disapproval in his drink.

He was not a bad-looking boy with his thin, olive-dark body and long, sad, slanting eyes, his delicate wrists and dark tapering fingers with their beautifully manicured nails sparkling white in contrast. His handsome features, however, were marred by a scar running down the length of one cheek.

They moved away into the shadows, obviously to avoid his scrutiny, and he felt suddenly neglected, left in limbo, miserable and alone. He finished his drink and attacked the peanuts in an effort to conceal his discomfort at being deserted in full view of the young Asian students or drop-outs who obviously considered him an intruder, if not a spy, in their mad, chaotic world.

He was wondering whether he should get up and leave and let Naoko find her own way back to the hotel, when there was a sudden commotion at the far end of the room. Looking up, he was just in time to see Naoko confronting her young man in what could only be a state of outrage. Raising her arm, she stepped back and slapped him with all her strength across the face.

Joe, secretly congratulating her for having come to her senses, dropped a thousand-yen note on the table, and pushed back his chair, grateful for the excuse to leave. However, the scene apparently had not come to an end. Before Naoko could turn her back on her partner, he retaliated by slapping her face in return.

This was quite a different matter. No Jap was going to strike his step-daughter, whether she deserved it or not, and Joe quickly went to her rescue. With one jab of his fist he floored the youth, who lay on his back, blood spurting from his nose. For a moment he lay staring unbelievingly at the dripping blood. Then with a spluttered oath he sprang to his feet, backed up now by several of his companions.

They grabbed Joe by the neck, the waist, and his feet and started beating him up, methodically, while the girls looked on, their screams drowned out by the blaring of the speakers. It was therefore with immense relief that Joe looked up from his struggles to find the room filled with police.

He remembered how considerate they were in the old days, how they cooperated with the foreigners almost to the point of embarrassment. When the youth and his companions had been subdued, Joe wiped his face with his handkerchief, said, 'Well, thank God you fellows showed up! Don't be too tough on the lads. A couple of days in the jug should do the trick.'

The police sergeant said nothing. He motioned to his men, and Joe, Naoko, his assailant, ten youths and seven girls, were led outside and herded into an old three-wheeled van which

Joe remembered was used to round up prostitutes in Shimbashi. His wrists were handcuffed, and a policeman stood over him holding a gun big enough to kill a polar bear.

He managed to get close to Naoko and said incredulously: 'How can they get away with this? After all, we're American citizens!'

'You sound like an outraged hen who complains because she's broken her own eggs. You didn't have to hit the bloke, Daddy.'

'Nobody's going to slap your face, nobody!' he growled.

'It was my fault. I started it.'

'That's neither here nor there. Or is it? Why did you do it?'

'When he found I couldn't speak Japanese he was furious. He called me a traitor to my country – a typical product of American imperialism. He raved at me until I couldn't stand it any more! But he's awfully handsome! If he just hadn't gone on and on.'

'The bloody Communist! I'll kill him. Now you know how your mother was treated – how she felt,' he said, and was silent.

Chapter Fifteen

Joe woke the next morning with a splitting headache. He was determined to find a quiet home outside Tokyo where he could settle down with Naoko for three months and get on with his work. His first evening in the city, though instructive, could not by any twist of the imagination, be considered a success, and though he had been given a suspended sentence for assault and battery, he had escaped spending the night in jail only by having to bow three times before the magistrate and, at his command, repeat 'So sorry, so sorry, so sorry'. It had been a humiliating experience, especially in front of the grinning Japanese police officers, but at the time it had seemed the only way out of a nasty situation.

The quiet seaside town of Kamakura where he had first met

124

and wooed Hanako was the most likely choice. He remembered the peaceful setting of the Buddhist sanctuary with its lotus ponds and temple bells with delight, almost with reverence, and after they had breakfasted in the Phoenix Room he called a taxi and they caught the train from Shimbashi.

Joe was pleased to see that the countryside – if one could call it countryside – had not altered very much. Wooden shacks still lined the rails, but in place of the men in white loincloths who handled the miles of crushed seaweed on the beaches, now thousands upon thousands of bathers swarmed over the sands like ants.

And Yokohama was once again a thriving metropolis, its tall buildings crowding the sky, its port crammed with shipping in the centre of which the old battleship *Mikasa* floated as a monument of the good old pre-war days.

As they approached Kamakura, Naoko asked, 'Does Grandpa live here?'

'No. Why? Would you like to meet him?'

'I don't care. I just wondered. What's he like?'

'A stubborn old man – a real Samurai! You should be pleased to be a member of such a distinguished family.'

'That's not what Mummy said.'

'She's prejudiced. After all, he disowned her.'

'Why, Daddy?'

'We won't go over all that again.'

'Where does he live?'

'In Kyoto.'

'Is that far from here?'

'It was. It used to take ten hours. Now, with the Limited Express, it takes about six.'

She was silent in thought.

'Yes, I'd like to meet him,' she said. 'Will you take me, please?'

'I'll take you one day if you insist,' he said. 'But I don't guarantee we won't be kicked out or arrested – if he's still alive, that is. I kidnapped you, don't forget. And after last night I don't want another encounter with the *keisatsu*!'

Deep down he was probably prepared to be disillusioned,

even though he wouldn't admit it. For one thing he learned that the schools of esoteric Buddhism such as the Tendai Sect and the Shingon Sect which had once prospered in Kamakura had now been replaced by new schools appealing to the masses. The little curio stalls and antique shops that had once been pitifully empty of their *objets d'art* were now overflowing with hideous souvenirs, surrealistic drawings, imitation jewellery, postcards, and Japanese screens painted by the local hacks who thrived on it.

They climbed to the hill-top where Hanako had lived and where they were married, but the shrine had disappeared and in place of the row of little wooden houses there now stood a golf club with eighteen holes of green turf stretching as far as the eye could reach.

It was obvious to Joe that he would not find his secluded workshop here and he returned to the village determined to impress Naoko at least with the Great Buddha in the Temple of Daibutsu. He remembered how he had stood silently before it in the moonlight and how its magic and mystery had strangely affected him. But now again he was disappointed, for the temple was filled with tourists snapping photographs, and coach after coach drove up to the front gate discharging their load of schoolchildren dressed in uniform and carrying banners. They crowded the flagstones and footpaths sucking choc ices and sweets. Joe was reminded of the zoo in New York's Central Park, and as Naoko was plainly bored, he surrendered to her suggestion to have lunch and went in search of the Japanese wayside restaurant which had once served him such a generous meal when the villagers had little or nothing to eat themselves. But he found that the *ryoriya* had been sold and in its place stood an impressive French restaurant catering to the foreign residents who flocked to Kamakura to avoid the crush of Tokyo.

They finally chose a small bar which served a set lunch of raw fish and *tempura*. It certainly was raw, the lobster so agonisingly alive that its feelers frantically pounded the plate while they picked away at the 'deelicious' thin slices of its body. The other hors d'œuvre consisted of several flat, round yellow fish which turned out to be jelly-fish. Upon learning this, Naoko very nearly vomited.

The fish seemed to be weighing on her mind all during the return trip to Tokyo. There was no doubt that she was feeling exceedingly uncomfortable, and once back at the hotel she went straight to bed.

'Daddy,' she moaned, 'I've got a terrible stomach-ache! It must be those horrible jelly-fish! Please give me a machine.'

'A machine? What are you talking about?'

'An enema. Mummy always gives me one when I have a stomach-ache. She calls it a machine because she can't pronounce it.'

'I see. Is it really that bad?'

'It's ghastly! It really is, Daddy!'

'Then I'll call a doctor. He'll give you a laxative.'

'No, *please*! I don't want a laxative. They give you piles. You have to have a terrible operation!'

'Where in the world did you get that idea!'

'Practically all the teachers in school have piles. Miss Map had a beastly operation. Afterwards she had to use a dildo three times a day to stop the wound from healing too quickly. Martha had to help her.'

'Martha?'

'She's number one in our biology class.'

'I see.' Joe hid a smile and scratched his head. 'Then I'd better find an American drug-store. I don't suppose Japan has ever heard of a machine, as you call it.'

'An enema, Daddy. And buy a bottle of witch hazel and some vaseline. Hurry. I think I'm going to be sick.'

When he returned with the instrument she was lying naked on her back, whimpering, a pillow over her face. He had never seen her naked, and he was shocked by the sheer beauty of her body, so like her mother's at twenty. He looked down at her, at the soft curve of her hips, the small dark crest of her loins, her full breasts with their firm pink nipples, and then aware of his presence, she sighed and rolled over on her stomach.

He removed a portrait of the Emperor from the wall above

127

the bed and hung the swollen plastic bag on the nail. After a moment of exploration he found the right channel – or prayed that he had – inserted the nozzle, and released the flood-gates.

'Please, Daddy, not so fast.'

He grabbed hold of the tube, squeezed it, then slowly released it again.

'All right?'

'Yes, Daddy.'

'How in God's name did your mother ever get mixed up with this kind of machinery?'

'Japanese doctors always gave her one when she was ill. They call it *kancho*, which means "water in stomach". It also means "government office",' she giggled.

'Stop that!' he roared. 'Keep still or there'll be a catastrophe!' Then finally, with a sigh of relief: 'Okay. That's that. The bag's empty. You'd better run for it.'

'One more, please, Daddy. And then I'll have a rest and you can have the night out on your own. I don't think I ever want to eat again.'

'You mean – good God, you're joking! Can you hold another bag?'

'I hope so – for your sake,' she giggled, and gritting her teeth, buried her head in the pillow.

When she was finally tucked under the covers with a hot-water bottle, Joe went around to the Press Club. He was eager to visit Shimbun Alley once again with its post-war memories, and curious to learn if any of the boys were still working in Japan for any of the news services. He also wanted to study the bulletin board for a possible furnished flat or house in Azabu, his second choice of residence now that Kamakura was out.

He discovered that the building had been torn down and in its place stood a miniature skyscraper. The club was on the first two floors and now consisted of three dining rooms, a theatre, bar, library and committee room.

He entered the bar which turned out to be a sumptuously carpeted lounge. It was crowded with small tables each with its own telephone extension. Men and women, Japanese and

128

American, sat drinking pink gins and old-fashioneds while they fingered news reports or rattled off their day's assignments over the wires. It was all very posh and efficient, but, for Joe, Shimbun Alley had completely lost its charm. None of the men were in shirt-sleeves and instead of girls in kimonos recruited from the tea houses in nearby Yuraku-chu, there were Japanese film stars and secretaries dressed in the latest Western fashion. Gone was the old bustle and ferment; in its place there exuded an atmosphere of ease and careless security, reeking of money and big business.

He saw no one he recognized and sat down on a stool at the bar beside two men bent over a leather dice cup on the counter. No sooner had he done so when the boy-san hurried over with a similar cup and placed it almost reverently in front of him.

'What's that for?' Joe asked, and pushed it aside.

And then he recognized the boy. Rather he was a 'man-san' now, his hair streaked with grey. But there was still the white coat and the tennis shoes to match.

'Kenzo! Well, for God's sake! Don't tell me you've been standing behind that bar for twenty years!'

'Barrett-san!' He reached across the counter and gripped Joe by the hand. 'Good to see you, sir! You still work for *Los Angeles Times*?'

'No, I'm afraid not. I'm gathering material for a book. Any of the old gang about?'

'Very few, sir. Mason-san came back with his wife and children. They live in Akasaka, but come in once a week to pick up mail.'

'Anybody else?'

'Can't think. Oh, yes – Garvan-san. He still works for UP. Came for Olympic Games and stayed on.'

'Good old Dennis! Where's he living?'

'At the Daiichi Hotel. But he away in Osaka. Come back two, three weeks. Oh, and Miss Conway is here.'

'Jane Conway! But that's impossible! She hated Japan – couldn't wait to get home. You mean she never left?'

'Don't know about that, Barrett-san. She secretary of club

now. Give everybody orders over phone from house. Come in once a month, maybe.'

'Well, I'll be damned!'

'I hear you married. To Japanese lady.'

'That's right. We live in London. I'm here with my daughter. We're looking for a furnished place in Azabu. Got any ideas?'

'Take a look at the bulletin board. Plenty places for rent this time of year. Americans leave Tokyo for beach. You find place easy.'

'I hope so. Well, thanks, Kenzo. Join me in a Suntory on the rocks for old times' sake, and then I'll have a look.'

'No thanks, Barret-san. Miss Conway say boy-san no drink with customer.'

'Sounds like Conway! To hell with her. Pour the drinks, boy-san! And don't spare the horses!'

Chapter Sixteen

The agent for the house Joe wished to view in Azabu had his office in Hongo. On Saturday morning he and Naoko set out on foot to pick up the key. They were just approaching the district when they came upon a large gathering outside an ornamental wooden gate. Curious as to what was going on, they pushed their way through the crowd into a walled square surrounded by red-brick buildings which Joe recognized at once as Tokyo Imperial University.

No sooner had they stepped into the square than they realized they were caught up in a militant student demonstration. Two or three hundred students in blue and yellow and white helmets were shouting slogans and waving their fists at an elderly Japanese man standing on the steps, obviously the President, who was trying to reason with them.

To no avail. The shouting persisted, grew more militant and savage. A flagstone flew through the air. The President ducked

130

and ran up the steps, pursued by the students. He managed to reach the door, slipped through it, and disappeared. The students, roaring vengeance, swarmed up the steps in pursuit. Finding the door locked, they proceeded to attack it with rocks and wooden staves. Bricks and concrete paving crashed through the windows. A shock brigade forged their way head first into a classroom, smashing what remained of the broken panes with their helmets.

A whistle shrilled. Joe spun round to find a squad of riot police descending upon them, brandishing truncheons and waving shields. He turned back and saw that the students, warned of the attack, had faced about and, with staves raised, were rushing forward to counter-attack. Joe and Naoko, innocent bystanders, were caught between the two warring factions.

Joe grabbed Naoko by the arm, but at that very moment the two forces met and clashed. He lost his grip on her as he was knocked off his feet, and fell to the pavement. He was aware of being trampled by heavy hobnailed boots, kicked, and beaten, and then mercifully darkness closed in on him.

When he regained consciousness he was lying on the grass in a corner of the square. The battle was still in full swing. Naoko was nowhere to be seen.

He struggled to his feet, looking desperately around for help, but the police were too occupied to take any notice of him, and in a way he was relieved, not wanting to be hauled to jail a second time in one of their three-wheeled vans or be taken for a casualty and hustled into one of the waiting ambulances.

And then he saw her. She appeared out of the mêlée in the arms of a blue-helmeted student who carried her to the grass sanctuary and deposited her shaken, but smiling, at Joe's feet.

'Naoko! Are you all right?'

'Quite all right, Daddy. Thanks to Naruhito. I was knocked down by a policeman who thought I was going to punch him. I wish I had! I might have been killed. Naruhito saved my life!'

'Naruhito?' He turned to the student, mumbled: 'Thanks, my boy.' And then to Naoko: 'Come, let's get out of here before we're both slaughtered.'

It was not until the student had removed his helmet, bowed, and run back to join his comrades that Joe recognized the youth with his thin, olive-dark face marred by its scar, his gleaming white teeth, his long, sad, slanting eyes which blazed now with revolutionary fervour.

The house in Azabu was on a hill-top immune from earth-quakes and floods overlooking a cluster of small shops and the Inari shrine. Joe found it comfortable as well as a stimulus for his work because, though the two bedrooms were Western style, the living room and bath were authentic Japanese. He moved his notes and reference books into the living room and worked on a long, low lacquer table, his feet stretched out beneath, his back braced by a wall of silk cushions.

A week passed, and in spite of the summer heat, he worked well, gathering together his material under chapter headings during the daytime, and exploring the various restaurants with Naoko at night. She did not disturb him during the day, and though he felt guilty at times, realizing he was neglecting her, he knew she understood he had a job to do, and went out sight-seeing on her own.

At least that was how he imagined she occupied herself. It was not until he happened to drop in to one of the cafés at the bottom of the hill for a cup of green tea that he discovered otherwise. Sitting at a table by the window, he found her, to his utter amazement, deep in conversation with the Japanese student.

He strode up to her, ignored the boy, and demanded: 'What are you doing here? I thought you were going to the museum.'

'I changed my mind,' she said gaily. 'Rather Naruhito changed it for me. We've been walking in the park and dropped in here for a cup of tea on my way home. Sit down and join us, Daddy.'

He ignored her request. 'How did you happen to meet? I thought after insulting you and the trouble we had with the police, this . . . this Marxist would be the last person you'd wish to see again!'

'Oh, that's all forgiven and forgotten. I went to the university

132

to thank him for saving my life, and he apologized. He'd had a bad day and drank a whole bottle of *sake*.'

'I see.' Joe turned to the boy, who stood up and bowed, but did not speak. There was a smirking, arrogant smile on his lips which Joe would have liked to wipe away with his fist, but decided against it. He had had enough brushes with the police during his sojourn in Japan.

'Look, whatever-your-name-is,' he scowled. 'I have nothing against you personally, but I don't want you to see my daughter again, d'you hear? She's a schoolgirl – well, she's just finished school, and we're returning to London in a few weeks. I don't want her involved in any more of your violent protests or whatever you're up to out there at the university. Now if you don't mind . . .'

The young man stood up and gave a stiff, ironical bow, turned on his heel, and walked away, graceful as a tom-cat.

'Daddy! Don't be beastly! Naru's done nothing to hurt me – on the contrary, he's been kind and very helpful.'

'Naru? So it's come to that? You mean this is not the first time you've been out together?'

She glanced down at the table, said: 'Only once or twice.'

'Well, that's the end of it.'

'But I want to go out with him! Why shouldn't I? You're horrible! And we have a date tomorrow to go to the movies.'

'I'm sorry, but I've made other arrangements.'

'What arrangements?'

'To visit your grandfather,' he said on the spur of the moment. 'It was your wish. We leave on the nine o'clock train in the morning. Now finish your tea.'

The Limited Express was quite a change from the crowded post-war local that stopped at every station to take on shabby passengers in Army puttees and straw sandals, weighted down with their gigantic bundles. Though the train was crowded, there were plush seats for all, tilted as on an airliner with padded foot-rests, earpiece radio units, and radio-telephone communication with Tokyo and Osaka. In the restaurant, where they had breakfast, there was a speedometer that registered over a hundred miles an hour, and in place of the push trolleys serving *sake* and sweets, now they served French champagnes, Italian liqueurs, Scotch whisky, and food prepared by the Imperial Hotel chef.

They settled back over their coffee and scrambled eggs listening to Beethoven's Fifth Symphony over the loudspeaker and watching the villages fly by. Fuji, with its wide skirt and high cone, was not visible in the haze of the summer heat, but they saw occasional glimpses of the sea, though now and then, where once rice paddies had held the whole of the sky mirrored on their surfaces, great new factories sprang into sight with their endless dormitory dwellings and schools for the workers' children, sanatoriums, playing fields and netted golf ranges.

Perhaps because Naoko was sulking when he hoped she would fall in love with Kyoto as he had done, breathtaking and majestic as he remembered it, he found it rather disappointing. To be sure, the old capital was full of impressive temples, gardens and shrines of immortal beauty, but now boasting over a million inhabitants, and half as many cars, it had somehow lost its serenity, elegance, and magic. No sooner had they left the station than they were set upon by long-haired demonstrators wearing square sunglasses shouting slogans through portable loudspeakers. Joe caught a few of the words, like 'Okinawa' and '*Amerikajin*' – 'Americans go home', and hurried off down the main street.

It was no longer wide and sun-filled, but overcast with a grey-yellow haze. A bitter chemical smell rose from the new industrial zones centred on the city. In place of the exquisitely dressed young ladies who had walked the romantic old passages peering into the wayside shrines inhabited by cooing doves, swarms of pedestrians choked the sidewalks as they hurried past the big department stores, bookshops, fashionable boutiques, through the crowded arcades crammed with cameras, colour TVs, golf clubs, electronic calculators and juke boxes. Most of them wore small white masks over their noses and mouths to protect them from the smog.

Joe hailed a taxi and instructed the driver to take them to Kinugasa Hill. He did not know Morimoto's address, but once they had arrived in the lovely wooded district with its land-scaped gardens and ancient temples he was sure he would recognize the house. After all, it was one of the most beautiful in the neighbourhood.

They arrived at the foot of the hill, and though the temples and the park were still there, there were no homes at all. In their place stood a modern hotel surrounded by driving schools and yet more netted golf ranges. Flabbergasted and deeply concerned, Joe asked the driver: 'But Mr Morimoto lived right there! In a big house with a garden and a rock pool! What's become of it – of him?'

'Morimoto-san? Former Director of National Museum?'

'That's right. I visited him just after the war.'

'Ah, so! He very old man. Government buy this land many years ago. Force owners to sell. Think maybe he live in city now. I try to find.'

They drove back several miles and turned off into a small segregated district where women were washing clothes in an open roadside ditch. The area swarmed with noisy children and people pulling hand-carts in from the side streets. Finally they reached a canal bordered with willow trees. Rusty brown houses backed against it in an endless row. There was no smog, how-ever, and the stones in the river-bed shone with colour from the unstitched and drying kimonos draped over them.

The driver climbed out and spoke to the children. He re-turned in a moment and pointed to one of the houses. 'Mori-moto-san live there. Thank you.'

At the gate Naoko said: 'Grandpa lives here!'

'It does seem strange. He was a very rich man. I don't under-stand it.'

He knocked on the door, and then a second time. There was a shuffling of slippered feet, and a quavering voice asked: *'Dare desuka? Nanno goyodesuka?'*

'My name is Joe Barrett. I've brought your grand-daughter to see you, Mr Morimoto.'

After a long pause the door slid open and a bent figure with a wilderness of white hair and a flowing white beard, wearing a faded grey kimono with a long sash knotted below his waist, appeared before them squinting through narrowed lids, one hand over his eyes to shield them from the glare of the sun.

'Barret-san?' he asked. Each word seemed to have been dragged from the depth of his thin, withered body, from a past long forgotten, yet faintly familiar, and somehow urgent.

'That's right. And this is your grand-daughter, Naoko.'

'Naoko?'

'Don't you remember? I kidnapped her while she was asleep in your garden. Twenty years ago. I thought you'd like to see how she's grown. We're here on a visit.'

'Naoko?' He shuffled up to her, staring at her face, one trembling hand exploring her chin, her hair, her eyes. 'Naoko. *Anata kane?*'

'I'm afraid she can't speak Japanese,' Joe said, embarrassed. 'May we come in?'

'*Dozo!*'

They took off their shoes and he led the way down a narrow passage into an eight-mat room covered with cream *tatami*. The only furnishings were a lacquer table, a small shrine in one corner, and a dresser upon which rested his two dead sons' portraits edged with black velvet. In the *tokonoma*, instead of the customary scroll and vase of flowers, hung two of the priceless black ink paintings which had formed part of the collection which had once adorned the corridor of his former spacious home.

He motioned them to sit down on the cushions around the table, then went into the kitchen to prepare tea. When he returned with the tray he set it down on the table and said: 'You must forgive me. I have no maid, and my niece who looks after me does not come to the house until the evening.'

'You've moved,' Joe said, as Morimoto settled himself on a cushion in front of them.

He smiled wanly. 'It is not as large or as comfortable as my ancestral home. It is sufficient, however, for an old man who must live alone. My wife died ten years ago.'

'Daddy has spoken often about your lovely house,' Naoko said. 'You must miss it dreadfully.'

'Of course. It was my intention that you should inherit both my house and my estate at the death of my sons, but the gods have planned it otherwise. You left Japan, and after the Government saw fit to requisition my home, my nephew fell into debt. I did what I could to save him from disgrace, but everything I possessed has been sacrificed.'

'I'm sorry to hear that,' Joe said.

'It is of no consequence. I shall not be in this world much longer. I am quite content to live out my days here in quiet contemplation.' He sipped his tea, his hand now surprisingly steady as he balanced the cup in his palm. 'You are living in America, Barrett-san?'

'No, in England. I've come to Japan for a few weeks on business.'

'You find it changed?'

'I certainly do! I'm amazed. I remember you saying that after the war Japan would return to its earthly paradise, to the old traditions of the divine age.' He grinned. 'And I said I thought you could expect some surprises!'

Morimoto smiled indulgently. 'It is true. But I also said, I believe, that Japan had not been wholly conquered – that it had a great future. These changes you speak of, our skyscrapers, our industrial and economic progress are but monuments to that prophecy. Our humiliation and sense of guilt and inferiority have been eradicated. We have borrowed from the West, we have copied you, because knowledge is imitation. To learn we must imitate. But now there is nothing more for Japan to learn from the West.'

'But is this new confidence, this new aggressiveness, all for the good, sir? In your opinion? I remember you felt that Japan would once again shut itself into a shell – wouldn't permit foreigners with their alien customs and know-how to open it again.'

'It was forced upon us by the war, was it not? It is said that the Occupation GIs carried samples of America's latest products and technology in their kit-bags when they arrived on our shores! We have used them to our own advantage, have become an economic super-power, and because of it a process of decay has already begun to set in.'

137

'I haven't seen any sign of it,' Joe said sceptically.

'Humility has given way to arrogance. A coldness and strangeness have entered our lives. Our big industrialists who brought change to our islands, superimposing your culture on ours, believing that change is life, have come to learn that change is also death, bringing about its own extinction. We stand now in the same position as our ally Germany did in 1938.'

'You mean you think there'll be another war – that your new nationalism will lead to new militarism?' Joe asked, alarmed.

'No, no. We have copied your dress, your tall buildings, your parliaments, your railroads, your taxation system, but we shall not copy your nuclear bombs. We have learned of its evil. We have had enough. The industrialists have taken the place of our generals – those who could once ask for anything and get it. What I am saying to you is that the inflated balloon will one day burst. Already our Shinto religion, banned during the post-war years, is being taught again in our schools. Though we wear your suits and ties to conclude multi-million-dollar deals with you in computers or shipping, we come back here to our wooden houses and change into our national dress. In spite of our great prosperity, there is much impatience among the people who feel they are not getting a fair share of the money being earned. While our ancient obedience to regimentation will serve the leaders in power, the breaking point is near. The accumulation of so much wealth is simply God's means to a roundabout return to the old days, to our freedom, our elegance, our privacy.

'But come,' he said, placing his cup on the tray and turning to Naoko. 'I have been talking much nonsense and neglecting my grand-daughter. Well, it is best that we speak together in private. That is, my dear, if you will accept an old man's invitation to spend the night. You shall sleep here in this room. I am sure that Barrett-san will not be offended. There are excellent Western hotels only a short distance away. You do not speak Japanese, my child. We must remedy that if we can. After we have dined we shall have a lesson, and I shall teach you the rudiments of an ancient cult – flower arrangement.'

Naoko looked pleadingly at Joe, vehemently shaking her head. Joe ignored her and said: 'That's very kind of you, sir. Naoko would love to stay the night. A lesson in Japanese is just what she needs. If you'll excuse me now, I'll be on my way. And thank you for your courtesy – and the tea.'

He bowed and went to the door. Naoko followed him to the gate, still protesting.

'Daddy, please don't leave me. *Please*. I don't know what to say to him. I haven't any night clothes, not even a toothbrush. Please let me go back to Tokyo. *Please!*'

'He's your grandfather, Naoko. You'll probably never have another opportunity to see him alive.'

'But he's rude! He never asked about Mummy once!'

'He wouldn't. But he's an old man – you must find it in your heart to forgive him.'

He planted a kiss on her brow, and left.

Chapter Seventeen

It was his first free night in Japan since his arrival, and he wanted to make the most of it. He had no intention of spending the evening or even dining at the lavishly modern Western-style hotel where he was given a room with a double-spring-mattress bed, concealed strip lighting, and a sunken rock bath. He would go exploring, mix with the local Japanese, meet a girl perhaps, and try to recapture the old Japan he once knew.

After a snack at a bar in a narrow dark passage he chose a dance palace called the Cabaret Moonbeam. It was not a very good choice, he was soon to discover – it had once been a roller-skating rink for the Japanese Army – but it was obviously authentic and a far cry from the gaudy, expensive tourist clubs in Tokyo.

It had a slippery wooden floor with chairs and tables set on a raised dais. An orchestra played at the far end of the room under a Japanese flag. It consisted of a strange assortment of two guitars, an accordion, a piano, a saxophone, and a drum. Each musician wore a black sweater, and the drummer had a red beret.

The hostesses sat glumly on their chairs against the walls, some in slacks, others in evening gowns that looked as though they were made from curtain material. Some of them kept putting on lipstick and others primped their hair, but the majority only sat and stared straight ahead, their feet stretched out before them.

As Joe elbowed his way through the crowd, a girl bumped into him. He turned and looked at her. Her shoulder-length hair was streaked with red dye. Her face was old and caked white with make-up to give her youth. She winked and smiled at him and showed him a flash of her gold-capped teeth.

Some of the boys had brought their own girls. They sat on the boys' laps smoking and whooping and drinking from open bottles. They dangled their stubby legs while their partners pinched and felt them, laughing and shouting to one another. One or two had already passed out; several had been sick, and one boy lay with his cheek and hair in a puddle of spilt beer.

A small marmoset of a girl sidled up to Joe, her eyes popping out of her face. Her skinny, almost boyish body was clothed in a thin sweater and skirt.

'Yiu,' she pleaded. 'Dance – oo?'

'Sorry, I haven't bought any tickets,' he said.

'Uh-kay, just we dance-oo. Gimm' money, not chickett-o, uh kay?'

She had a scalding little body, sharp and bony, which she thrust against him as she danced. Her face was hot and damp with perspiration. He wondered if she were ill, or only excited. The music stopped, but she held herself tight against him, like a curtain against an open window. He felt no desire, only pity for her.

'Yiu,' she whispered, 'berry nice – oo. Fuast time you come dis kyabaray?'

'Yes, first time,' he said.

She dug her chin into his shoulder, her damp stray hair

rung the bell and, receiving no reply, had gone about her business, telling herself that no doubt the girl had left London for a stay in the country. After all, the weather was lovely, and what was the point of staying in the city with both Joe and her daughter away in Japan?

However, a week had gone by and still there was no sign of Hanako. Not only Midori, but Scott also was worried, and today she was determined to find out if Hanako was away or merely playing possum.

She rang the bell, but again there was no answer. The curtains were drawn, and there were three bottles of milk standing outside the door. After a moment of deliberation, she went to the window, found it was unlocked, raised it, and stepped over the sill into the bedroom.

It was empty, but in terrible disorder, the bed unmade, the blankets strewn over the floor, spilled powder scattered on the carpet. The clock on the mantel had run down; its hands pointed to ten past seven.

Naoko's bedroom was clean and spotless, as she had left it.

But the kitchen was also in shambles, unwashed dishes piled in the sink, stale slices of bread and jam lying open to the flies on the breakfast table, a broken egg on the floor, a water tap running.

Midori found her in the living-room. She was slumped in a chair in her nightdress, her eyes closed, an empty bottle of Scotch by her side. Her hair was filthy and matted, her feet bare. She looked thin and emaciated.

After one glance Midori crossed to the desk and picked up the phone. She dialled a number, waited, and said: 'Scott? I'm at Hanako's flat . . . Yes. You'd better come over at once . . . Ten minutes? That will just give me time to bathe her and get her into some clean clothes.'

Scott pushed open the door and glanced about the room, frowning. It was empty, but down the hall he could hear voices, interspersed by the rush of a hand shower and shrieks of protest.

143

He took note of the condition of the flat, how the dust covered every item of furniture except one chair, the books and magazines lying open on the sofa, the hi-fi records piled on the radiogram, the empty bottle of Scotch on the table.

He went over and examined it. As he did so, a letter concealed under the bottle came unstuck and floated to the floor. He picked it up, saw that it was from Naoko in Japan, and read:

Dearest Mummy:

Well, here we are in Tokyo, the most *fabulous* place I've ever seen! We stopped at the Imperial Hotel, but Daddy wanted to get down to work, so we moved to this *fabulous* house in Azabu. We tried Kamakura where you were married, but it wasn't very nice. Daddy took me to see the Great Buddha, which was *fabulous*, it really was, and I just loved the little art shops full of these *kokeshi* dolls and Japanese screens. But we went to a nasty little café called a *nomiya* (see how well I can speak Japanese?) where they served us raw jelly-fish, can you believe it! I was so sick I thought I would die! Daddy had to give me a machine. He was petrified I couldn't hold it. I didn't tell him you always gave me three bags and then took me to a movie afterwards. I pretended I was tired and he put me to bed with a hot-water bottle! Imagine! In this heat! Poor Daddy. He really is a poppet, though a bit square at times.

He misses you, Mummy. He misses you a lot. He doesn't talk about it, but I can tell because when we go out he always takes me to places where you've been twenty years ago! He doesn't seem to realize that Japan has changed. He just won't accept it. I don't believe you'd recognize it either. How silly of you not to come with us! You and Daddy could go to all the dreadfully dull geisha shows and museums together while I went out with Nahurito.

Oh, I forgot! I haven't told you about Naru, have I? Oh, Mummy, he's *fabulous*. He's a student at Tokyo Imperial University and belongs to the *Zengakuren*, whatever that is. They're trying to get rid of the present government, the

144

Americans, and the establishment. They held a big demonstration the other day, and the riot police . . .

Footsteps sounded in the corridor. Scott hurriedly replaced the letter, then turned to face his wife, followed by Hanako, who gave him a sour smile and sank into the chair which obviously had become her permanent abode. She glanced at the empty bottle, struggled to her feet, and found herself helpless in Scott's embrace.

'Oh, no you don't. You've had enough of that poison.'

She fell back into the chair, her hands over her eyes. She was still in a daze; time and place meant nothing to her. Obviously she was reliving the letter she had received from Naoko.

'I've spent all my life teaching her that Japan isn't her home,' she said bitterly. 'I've tried to purge myself of what the Japanese did, what my husband did, how my father-in-law treated us. That a daughter of mine should go back and like it is just too much! I wanted her to hate it – that's why I let her go . . .'

'That's enough,' Scott said sternly. 'Japan's no longer your home, nor mine. You're living in England now, and you're leaving this flat and coming to stay with us. Midori, take her into the bedroom and help her pack her things. I'm going to the High Street to fetch a cab.'

Seated alone with Hanako in the library of his town house in Chester Square, Scott drained his cup of black coffee and gave Hanako his full and undivided attention.

'Now listen to me,' he said. 'I'm going to talk to you as Joe should have done twenty years ago. You've got to snap out of it. Joe loved you or he wouldn't have married you. He could have married a hundred eligible girls in the States, but he didn't. He went all the way to Japan and chose you. All these years he's tried to give you everything he thought you wanted. And what have you given him? A bloody rotten time.

'Joe's still a young man. I know you've had a rough deal, but so did most of us during and after the war. Look at Midori – does she lock herself in her room and harp on the past? It was just as hard on her as it was on you when you first came to London.'

'Don't please! I know how silly I've been. But I was afraid of losing Joe.'

'That's just what you're going to do.'

'I've gone through so much. I can't forget it, I can't!'

Scott pulled up a chair, said: 'Do you love Joe?'

'He's my whole life.'

'Have you, in the eighteen years you've been married, ever stopped to think that a man's horizons are always wider than a woman's? If you had married a racing driver and then refused to let him enter a race because you loved him so much – made him give up racing – would you have kept his love? No, you would have destroyed him, as you're destroying Joe. You've got to give him freedom to live in his own way. For eighteen years you've done it your way. I think it's his turn now.'

She did not reply, merely stared at the floor. Scott sighed and got up from his chair.

'I want you to meet a friend of mine,' he said.

'I don't want to meet anyone!' she cried. 'I want to go home.'

'This is your home until Joe comes back. That is, if he ever does.' He opened the door, said: 'Come in, Michael. This is Hanako Barrett. She's staying with us while her husband is in Japan. You two might like to have a chat. I'll make a fresh cup of coffee.'

She looked up and saw a tall, angular Englishman with thinning blond hair smiling down at her. She felt his awkwardness, and his gentle, shy manner caused her once again to cover her face with her hands.

He, in turn, saw a Japanese lady dressed in a shapeless gown with deep circles under her eyes. Her hair, streaked with grey, was tucked in tight coils at the nape of her neck. Her cheeks were stained with tears.

He sat down beside her, and said: 'Scott has told me about you and Joe. I don't suppose I can be of any help – it would be presumptuous of me to even think I could – but I thought I'd tell you that I've just returned from Japan. It was my first visit,

146

and I found it one of the most interesting, one of the most beautiful, one of the most progressive countries in the world.'

'You went as a tourist,' she protested. 'You know nothing of what I know – how stupid and cruel the people are – how callous, how selfish, how brutal. You saw only what they wanted you to see. You don't know how evil they can be!'

'I have a pretty good idea,' he said with a smile, and, getting to his feet, unbuttoned his shirt in front of her.

She glanced up and screamed. From his throat to his navel his body was covered in scars, some of them deep hollows which had never healed, purple-white and cavernous.

'I was a Japanese prisoner-of-war for three years in a camp in Singapore,' he said. 'I never quite understood how, in our time, there could be so many different ways of killing people without shooting them. What you see here was the result of Japanese soldiers having bayonet practice on live prisoners tied to trees or between bamboo posts. Fortunately I managed to escape – and survive.'

'Oh, please!' Hanako pleaded. 'I don't want to hear. Haven't I told you . . . ?'

'I don't want to upset you,' he said, buttoning his shirt and sitting down opposite her again. 'I just want to say that even at our worst moments in prison our fellows didn't have any personal feelings against our captors because we knew they were only puppets of a huge, impersonal force. They didn't know what they were doing. Or if they did, it was only because they were instruments of a kind of accumulated revenge of history on the European for his invasion of the East and his arrogant assumptions of superiority. The pent-up flood of resentment following centuries of frustration had simply broken through restraints. You understand what I'm saying? We forgave them their sins for they knew not what they did.'

She did not reply, and after a time he took her hand and said: 'Mrs Barrett, I'd like you to do me a favour. I happen to be Secretary of the Japan Society here in London. We're holding a gathering for our members on Wednesday in Hampstead to demonstrate flower arrangement. Midori will preside, but she's desperately in need of an assistant. Will you be kind enough – and sensible enough – to come to the meeting and help us out? I think you'll find that our members are not all ogres. In fact, I think you'll be pleasantly surprised.'

Again she was silent. He saw the struggle that was taking place in her mind, saw the little lines about her eyes and mouth deepen and tighten, and said: 'Well, Mrs Barrett?'

After what seemed an age, she whispered: 'I . . . I'll think about it,' jumped up, and ran from the room.

Chapter Eighteen

Joe picked Naoko up outside her grandfather's house at nine o'clock the next morning. The old man was still asleep, and Naoko had been waiting impatiently beside the gate for Joe to appear. He said nothing until they were in the taxi on their way to the station.

'Well, how did it go?'

'Not too badly. I was furious when you left me alone with him. I didn't know what to say. But then his niece came to cook dinner and we took a walk along the canal. He's really a dear old thing, but he still wouldn't talk about Mummy. He talked about his sons and Grandma, about Japanese art, the Kabuki, the Nō plays, and the tea ceremony!'

'I'm glad. He's a very knowledgeable old man. There aren't many left like him in Japan.'

'Thank heaven for that! I know I shouldn't have been bored, but I was. He reminds me of the silly Lords and Ladies in England who try and hold on to their glorious past, their empires, their great estates. You know, like Blenheim and Chatsworth. Only in Japan, at least in Tokyo, you sense that the new generation is sick to death of all that and are trying to build a new life. In England they don't care. They're just tired and lazy. They don't go to work until ten in the morning and quit at five. In Tokyo the little workshops are lit all night . . . '

'I suppose you're thinking of Naruhito's age group,' Joe said grimly.

'I wasn't, but now that you mention him . . .'

'I'm sorry, it was a mistake.'

'Dear Daddy,' she laughed. 'Who in this modern age wants to bother about tea ceremonies!'

'A great many people,' he said, 'It's one of the most important and impressive historical rituals in Japanese life.'

'Oh, my God!'

'It's an aesthetic communion service. A service in which worldly values are set aside, and minds and hearts consecrated to search for the beautiful, the good, the true, and the eternal.'

'You *are* joking. You should have been a Buddhist priest!'

'Through inner purification the tea-cultists learn how to refine their thinking. They develop such keen powers of discernment that they're able to find beauty and inspiration in things that most humans consider ugly and repellent. They drink tea, of course, but that's a minor part of the ceremony. The real objective is to clear the inner vision, to move upward and outward towards perfection.'

'Daddy dear! What *did* you do last night? You sound as if you have a guilty conscience, trying to atone for some horrible orgy. Shame!'

'I think a lesson in tea-ceremony is just what you need!' he said angrily. 'A taste of aesthetics might cleanse your mind.'

'No, thank you. I've had quite enough for one night!'

'Nevertheless,' he said obstinately, 'you're going to see a side of Japan you haven't seen before. A far cry from Tokyo or Kyoto. We're going to spend the night in a little fishing village where the Amas dive for pearls. It's called Wagu. If you're a good girl maybe the manager of the farm will give you a sacred black pearl to wear over your dispassionate heart.'

'Daddy,' she cried, 'you are a bore! You really are.'

Joe was certain, beyond a doubt, that Wagu had remained untouched, situated, as it was, at the tip of the Izu peninsula and accessible only by a winding, pocked, dirt road. He was wrong. No sooner had they stepped from the bus than they were

149

confronted by a five-storey hotel boasting two hundred bed-rooms, roof garden, sky restaurant, convention hall, and parking lot for fifty cars. It stretched along the hill-top overlooking the calm inlet which was now empty of its cryptomeria rafts, though fishing boats and cabin cruisers were plentiful, tied up at the wharf.

'It looks rather attractive,' Naoko said, pleasantly surprised. 'Could I do with a bath! And I'm starving! Let's eat and see if they have a discothèque in the village.'

Joe said furiously: 'I didn't bring you here to dance! And if you think we're going to spend the night at that hotel you're crazy. This is where we're staying.'

He nodded to the small wooden inn tucked away between the fishermen's shacks where he had stayed with Hanako. It hadn't changed in the least. He remembered vaguely that it had its disadvantages, but he didn't care; he had come back to Wagu to show Naoko a bit of rural Japan, and he wasn't going to be dissuaded. He walked across the street and knocked on the door.

He didn't really expect to be welcomed by the bewhiskered old lady in her grey kimono who had greeted him twenty years before, and was therefore not surprised when a younger woman bowed and escorted them in. She did seem taken aback, how-ever, when he asked for a room for the night. In her broken English she explained that they would be happier perhaps at the government-registered tourist hotel but he assured her they wouldn't and, with Naoko in tow, followed her to a room on the second floor.

'You don't remember me,' he said, 'but I paid a visit here many years ago. I was on the third floor overlooking the bay. Perhaps . . .'

She bowed and led him to the small five-mat room which he recognized at once. Nothing had been altered. A tiny naked light bulb still hung from the ceiling, and, if anything, the *tatami* was more soiled than before. The panes were still missing from the glass *shoji*.

'Lovely!' he said. 'Thank you very much.'

When the girl had left them alone, Naoko faced him with an expression of utter incredulity.

'You're joking! You're not going to make me spend the night here in this pigsty!'

'It's Japanese style,' he said, grinning. 'There's room enough for a family of ten.'

'And what's that awful smell!' she gasped. 'Oh, Daddy, I'm going to be sick!'

'Nonsense. That's the *benjo*. The bath is on the first floor, next to the kitchen. Would you like a quick soak?'

'In the sea, yes,' she said, and ran out of the house.

He followed her through the maze of fishermen's shacks, and then on to the breakwater. In front of the pearl farm she slipped off her dress and dived into the bay. He sat down and watched her swim around, her hair floating about her head in a wide dark halo, and for a moment his imagination played tricks with him. It could have been Hanako out there. The naked, gleaming body in the water was the same as Hanako's when they had bathed together in Lake Hakone. It seemed like yesterday.

A tear fell on his cheek. What a pity she wasn't here now – the three of them. What had gone wrong, that she had refused to come with them to her homeland? The fact remained that she was not here – that she would never return, and soon he would have to think seriously of what he was going to do. One thing he felt certain of: life with Hanako as he had known it had come to a dead end.

A Japanese fisherman appeared at his side and stood watching Naoko with obvious delight. His hands, tanned almost to blackness, were covered with wrinkles and old fishing scars, marks of the years he had spent in his trade.

'Wife?' he asked with a toothless grin.

'No, daughter.'

'Ah, so! Very good swim. Like Ama.'

'Where are the Ama girls?' Joe asked. 'What's happened to the pearl rafts that used to be here? And the farm workers?'

'All gone. Farm closed. Pearl market very, very bad. Say because American lady no wear pearls now. Wear hippy dress, *ne*?'

'So that's it. Pity.'

'*Dozo?*'

'The way fashions change. The way life changes. Nothing ever remains the same. Pity.'

The man rubbed his chin, coughed, and shuffled off to the village.

They dined at the tourist hotel because Naoko insisted upon it. 'If we have to go back to that filthy place I'm going to stuff myself with food until I fall asleep at the table,' she said.

Joe didn't follow her example; in fact he ate very little, but drank a great deal. He felt miserable, lonely, disillusioned. Nothing had turned out as planned. His last paradise had been desecrated, and all he wanted to do now was to return to Tokyo and get on with his work.

By the time they reached the Japanese inn, Naoko was nearly asleep, and Joe was so unsteady on his feet he had to be helped up the stairs. The bed rolls were laid out together on the *tatami* in the centre of the room beneath the naked light bulb, and two kimonos, gifts from the management, hung on pegs on the wall. Without further ceremony they threw off their clothes, climbed under their respective quilts, and fell into a deep sleep.

Surprisingly, after so many drinks, Joe had a happy dream. He was lying on the beach watching the Ama girls diving for pearls in the clear blue sea. Close by, other girls dried themselves over their brush fires, their white jackets drawn over their shoulders, exposing a wide expanse of chest. One of them, her hair dripping with salt water, smiled and came towards him carrying a wooden bucket filled with her morning's catch. He returned her smile, and she fell upon her knees beside him, her wide eyes questioning, inscrutable. Helplessly he stared at the loveliness of her mysteriously white breasts, polished by the salt waves, the skin of which was as transparent as lace. Then, lowering herself against him, she discarded her goggles and her tegane, and slipped off her shorts. He drew her to him, kissing her lips, his hands moving along the length of her spine and over the dark curled crest that awaited him.

'Daddy! Stop it! What are you doing!'

He opened his eyes, saw the first ray of dawn casting its shadow on the paper door, saw the girl naked beside him, her cheeks aflame, and gathered her into his arms. Her scent was sweet and fresh, and as he touched her smooth skin and heard her gasping breath, he felt his excitement running wild through his body.

'*Daddy!*'

The high-pitched scream shocked him into wakefulness. Instinctively he withdrew his arms and looked at his daughter, horrified and appalled.

'Daddy?'

He did not answer her.

'Do you want to make love to me – is that what's the matter?'

'Good God, no!' His heart was racing, his thoughts in a turmoil. His words came out in a breathless rush before he could control himself. 'Well, yes! Perhaps I did ... I was dreaming. I forgot you were my daughter. I ... '

'I'm not really, you know. I mean we're not even related.'

'Don't talk like that! Of course you're my daughter!'

She lay quite still beside him now, calm, no longer alarmed or apprehensive.

'I think I understand. I'm young and attractive, and you're lonely and mixed up. Isn't that it?'

'Obviously,' he said, feeling utterly ashamed, disgusted, revolted. With all the girls available to him in Japan, he had tried to rape his own daughter!

'I think I understand,' she said again. Her voice was low and very calm, and suddenly, it seemed, older, a little ominous. 'You're still in love with Mummy. That's why you brought me me here to this inn – to this very room where you made love to her when she was my age. You see her in everything you touch – even me.'

'No, no – you're wrong ... '

'And, Daddy ... Oh, I guess you don't want me to call you that any more.'

'Don't be an idiot!'

'There's another reason why I couldn't. I love you very much, but you're *old*. You're almost *forty-two*! You don't think you're old, but nobody ever does, do they? Not even when they're

153

fifty! That's why I can forgive you, why I feel sorry for you and Mummy, and all the unhappy, mixed-up, *sick* people there are in this world.'

He said, bristling: 'Forget it,' and rolled off her bed on to his own. 'I had too much to drink last night. It can happen to anyone,' he added belligerently. And then, after a silence: 'It's that boy, isn't it? Naruhito, or whatever-his-name-is.'

'It has nothing to do with him.'

'Then forget it,' he said again. 'I feel God damned bloody awful. I think I'm going to be ill.'

'Poor Daddy! We'd better catch the first bus home. When we get back I'll give you a machine.'

'Over my dead body!' he exploded, climbed to his feet, and reached for his clothes.

Chapter Nineteen

The weeks passed with Joe completely absorbed in his work, so absorbed that he received a severe shock when he happened to come across an unfinished letter from Naoko to her mother lying on her bedside table. He was shocked not only by its contents, but by the fact that she had written to Hanako at all. Because he had refrained from any contact himself, he had imagined that Naoko had done likewise.

Dearest Mummy:

Well, here I am again with the latest news, *fabulous* news! But first I'll go back a little. Daddy took me to see Grandfather in Kyoto. He's sold his big house and lives in a sweet little wooden cottage on the canal. Grandma died ten years ago and he's being looked after by his niece. He's a *fabulous* old man, he really is, and taught me all about Japanese art and the tea ceremony. I think he's lonely and misses you very much. I think he feels he made a great mistake not treating

154

you nicer when you were here. If only you could come and see him once before he dies. I'm sure you two would make it up, which would please Daddy who thinks he is a very learned man.

We went from there to Wagu on the Gulf of Izu where you stayed with Daddy. There's no more pearl diving, but we spent the night in the cute little inn where you stayed – in the very same room, in fact. Daddy pretended he didn't know it was the same room, but I knew he knew, and that's why he took me there. He was so homesick for you he got drunk and was sick all the way home on the bus.

Now for the *fabulous* news! You remember I told you about my boy friend, Naruhito? Well, I've been out with him every night for weeks. Daddy's so busy working he doesn't even know about it. And, Mummy – he proposed last night! I thought I would fall flat on my face because as a member of the *Zengakuren* he's supposed to despise Americans, have nothing to do with them. When I asked him about it he said once we were married I wouldn't be American any more. After all, I'm pure Japanese, aren't I? But I really think he's rather proud of his conquest, though he wouldn't admit it for the world. I mean the Americans did win the war and did look down on them, and I suppose he feels that he's getting back at us by marrying me! Actually, I chose *him*! I did, Mummy. He's so handsome, so sure of himself, so ambitious! Not to make money, he's against big business. He's head of the revolutionary student movement, which wants every student to take a leading role in the people's political struggles. I don't know what he's talking about half the time, but I love to listen to him. His eyes burn so brightly that I . . .

Joe dropped the letter as if it had been a hot coal. Had the girl gone mad! To want to marry a penniless Marxist – a militant revolutionary dedicated to the violent overthrow of the Government! He was out of his mind to bring her with him to Japan! He might have suspected something like this would happen. But of course it wasn't going to happen! He would see

155

to that. Hanako would have a heart attack if she received the letter. He tore it to shreds.

He regretted it afterwards because he would have to confront Naoko about the boy, and she would know he had read the letter and torn it up. Fortunately, or unfortunately, it never came to that. The next afternoon while he was hard at work she brought the idiot to the house and announced their intentions.

'There's nothing you can do about it, Daddy. We're going to get married at the end of term. So you two might just as well be friends.'

Joe sat across the table from the boy, slouched in a chair in his chequered shirt and jeans, and felt literally sick.

'I certainly can do something about it,' he said. 'I'm your father and you're under age . . .'

'You're not my father, remember? In Wagu . . .'

'All right, all right. But I'm in charge of you and you're going to do as I say. You're not going to marry this *anarchist*!'

'I think Grandpa might have something to say about that,' she said softly. 'He's my own flesh and blood and I'm sure he would approve.'

'May I ask, Mr Barrett, what you have against me?' the boy asked softly.

'If you don't know I see no reason to enlighten you. A penniless militant student with no prospects but to destroy everything that your country has built up over these past years! I don't even know your name!'

'Naruhito Sumitomo,' he said.

Joe paused in the middle of a fresh outburst. 'You're not related by any chance to Takashi Sumitomo, Chairman of the Sumitomo Shipping Company,' he said sarcastically.

'He's my father. Not that I'm proud of it. He has his life to lead, and I have mine.'

'You mean you want to destroy your own father! Everything he stands for? Isn't he a member of the Diet?'

'If you believe something is evil, Mr Barrett, it is only right to destroy it. That's what we believe.'

'You're insane! Violence will get you nowhere. You should know that.'

156

'I disagree. The Government's use of riot squads is violence. We resort to violence to challenge violence. Our armed demonstrations have the same significance as the guerrilla war in Vietnam. We don't consider student power as violence because we don't recognize the social order enforced by the State. If we feel that something is wrong – even if we don't understand the reason – we must resort to action. Through action we will come to understand what we had only felt was wrong, *is* wrong. We achieve nothing if we just say: "I don't understand". We don't fear the results of our action. What we fear is the cowardliness that denies us action.'

He spoke carefully, each word said as if he were recording for a tape machine for a replay to slow-witted people.

'But what do you *want*? To destroy the present establishments? What are you going to put in their place if you do destroy them?'

'Nothing.'

'Nothing!'

'We want to be free from the tyranny of the established order, free from the bureaucracy, the boss paternalism, the family paternalism which directs our lives from the womb to the grave. We want freedom from that discipline, from the old ones like my father who assume, because they are old, they have the key to success – to successful *living*.' He paused for a moment. His voice had been rising. Then he went on in chilling, quiet tones: 'Can *not* you old ones realize that dreams can be more real that waking thoughts? Can you not see also that *mind* is more important than *matter*?'

Joe interrupted: 'But of course I can, you young ape . . . '

'Then why are you so obsessed with matter, with materialism? We believe the youth of today knows better than the old ones, and can build a better world than the grey, rigid, conformist life which they have carved out for us without our consent – their colleges where we can only vaguely see through the mist the faces of our professors, the examinations which, if we fail, send us to the *pachinko* halls, or if we pass, to the dormitory in the factory of a company that chooses our wives, and where we stay singing lusty songs every morning and even-

157

ing until we retire. Is that what you want for Naoko, Mr Barrett? To be married to a robot?'

'Well, I don't think there need be any question of that. If it *did* come to that, Naoko would have an allowance – a dowry as you call it. And I assume you intend to pass your exams.'

'I shall pass them because I have been chosen by the selectors and they wouldn't dare fail me or they would lose face. And I must prove myself to be a responsible person, otherwise I could not continue to lead the student revolt. That does not mean, however, that I accept the Establishment, only that I shall be an individual to live my own life as I see fit.'

Joe looked down at his hands, feeling suddenly tired, confused, defeated. He just didn't understand the young man. He supposed he was one of the old ones, but he had no desire to be otherwise.

'Oh, Daddy, isn't he wonderful?' Naoko cried. 'You wait, you'll be proud of him one day!'

'I hope so, my dear. But I doubt it. I'm sorry, but I'm just not convinced. And as for your marriage, if you're serious, I'd write to your mother and ask her permission. I only hope the shock won't kill her.'

When they had gone on their way, Joe, feeling more depressed than he could ever remember, put aside his manuscript and took a taxi to the Press Club. He wanted to talk to someone, to anyone, even the boy-san, but he hoped that he might run into Dennis Garvan if he were back from Osaka. He was another of the old ones, part of the past; he might be able to buoy his spirits and straighten him out.

At the bar he learned from Kenzo that Garvan was expected back at eight o'clock that evening. He decided to have a few drinks, dine late, and be on hand when he arrived.

He had finished his third Scotch and soda when a voice over his shoulder caused him to spin round on the stool.

'Dr Livingstone, I presume! Well, this is a surprise! And all by your lonesome! I thought you'd have a litter of little Japs by now, all tagged with the American flag!'

'Jane Conway! You haven't changed a bit!'

'What did you expect? Ethel Barrymore in a wheelchair? You don't look a day older yourself.'

He was pleased to hear that. During the last few days, after his trip to Wagu, and his talk with Naru, he was beginning to feel like Methuselah's uncle.

She was very lovely, he had to admit, fresh and scintillating, in full possession of herself as well as several large diamond and emerald rings. Their reflection in the elliptical overhead lights nearly blinded him.

'Nice, aren't they?' she said with a flick of her wrist.

'You've struck oil, it seems.'

Her eyes twinkled. 'My father died five years ago.'

'Obviously it's not in the cards to say I'm sorry.'

'It's a little late for that. You should have said it when you left me for that little Jap nineteen years ago. What happened? Did you throw her into the Pacific?'

'She's in London. But let's not go over all that. It's good to see you again, Jane.'

He meant it. In his present mood she appeared like a goddess from the past, someone to reach out to in his loneliness and depression. The memory of her naked body lying without shame on the bed in the colonel's house, her breasts glowing like cream roses in the candlelight, swept over him with a wave of passion.

'Are you free tonight?' he asked.

'Could be. What have you in mind?'

'How about Shimbashi?' He grinned. 'I remember it had a certain attraction for you. Only don't do another striptease. I'm getting too old to be tossed out on the street.'

There was a sudden smile on her lips, but her eyes stared.

'You mean you want to pick up where we left off? Rather, where you left me off?'

'I don't see why not. Are you game?'

She slipped her hand into his, and he felt the softness of it, the firm clasp of her fingers in his, and shivered.

'Not Shimbashi,' she said, her cheek against his. 'I have a perfectly good home, and I don't feel hungry. Come, finish your drink. My car's parked in the alley.'

It was a blue Toyota 2000 GT sports model, and a beauty.

159

They roared through the streets behind the Palace to Sanban-cho, one of the most expensive districts in Tokyo, and pulled up in front of a long, low California-style house not far from the British Embassy.

'Well!' he said. 'You seem to have done yourself proud. I thought you didn't like Japan – how come you stayed on for so many years!'

'I went back once,' she said, 'to New York. It scared me to death. The whole country seemed to be falling apart, murders, strikes, demonstrations, while Japan was booming. Just after the war things were different. Now it's the most civilised country in the world. Come in.'

She led him up the steep steps into the house. He looked about him in amazement – at the plush Chinese carpet on the floor, the black and white leather furniture, the bound books that lined the walls, the enormous antique desk against the window stacked with papers – and whistled.

'You like my little hideaway?' she smiled, throwing off her wrap.

'You could no more hide here than you could in Grand Central Station!' he laughed.

She pushed him down on to the sofa amidst the largest cushions he had ever seen, then sat on his lap and threw her arms about his neck.

'Did you ever think about us – how it was – when you were with that Jap?' she smiled, kissing him hard on the lips.

'Don't let's talk about it,' he said, pulling her down beside him and trying to blot out Hanako from his mind, his thoughts, his body.

'I agree, darling,' she said, got up, and crossed the floor. 'I won't be a moment – don't run away.' She gave him a long slow glance, and entered what was obviously the bedroom. He waited, holding his breath in anticipation, prepared to give her time to undress as he had done when they had made love before.

He was just about to strip to his waist and go in search of her when the door opened and she returned, followed by a tall Japanese gentleman in a dark business suit and matching tie.

'I don't believe you've met Minoru, have you, Joe?'

'Minoru?' he muttered, struggling to his feet.

'My husband. Perhaps you've heard of the Ogihara Electric Industrial Company. Well, Minoru owns it.'

'Your husband?' Joe fell back on to the sofa.

'Joe Barrett was a reporter at the Press Club during the occupation days,' she informed Ogihara with a shrug.

Ogihara bowed. 'I'm glad to meet you, Mr Barrett. Please let me get you a drink.'

'No. No, thanks. I must be getting back. My daughter is waiting for me.'

'Your daughter? You didn't mention you had a daughter,' Mrs Ogihara said.

'No, silly of me, wasn't it? It never entered my mind.'

'I'm sure it didn't,' she smiled.

He got unsteadily to his feet and crossed to the door. 'I really must be going.'

He was furious with her and with himself. In a most vicious way she had made a fool of him. In a flash the image of Hanako hit him between the eyes, and vanished.

On the front steps he said bitterly: 'All right. You've had your revenge. What's it all about? You thought the Japanese were monkeys – gooks, as you called them. And now you're married to one. Why?'

'I told you. Japan is no longer a defeated or second-rate power. When my father died he left me penniless. Minoru is not only a rich man, but a handsome one and a model husband. Do you know what his yearly *income* is?'

'I don't give a bloody damn,' he shouted.

'Two million dollars! And please don't shout.'

She turned, still smiling, and went back into the house. The door snapped shut behind her.

Chapter Twenty

Dennis Garvan sat hunched in the chair, a drink in one hand, a stack of newspapers in the other. Though his shoulders were still massive and his thick black eyebrows showed not a trace of grey, his body seemed somehow shorter, less powerful, less aggressive.

Watching him while they filled in the years since their last meeting, Joe thought what a strange mixture of roughness and sensibility the man was. He seemed calm and composed, though tamed was a better word. Deep down inside he could have been seething, but something had put a stop to it, at least on the surface. Perhaps because his son had been killed in Korea, or because the recession in America had cost him his life savings – whatever it was it made him seem unsettled, insecure; yet the old poise, the pride, the arrogance were there. He'd been hurt, though he wouldn't admit it, and so he laughed, he appeared amused, he kept quiet, he acted tough, as he was.

'You're goddamned right things have changed,' he growled. 'I once told you the Americans should get the Japs to give up militarism and concentrate on economics. Well, unfortunately they followed our advice. And now we're trying to get them to reverse their decision – at least to the extent of spending some hard cash on their own defence.'

'Do you think they'll do it?'

'The hell they will! The Japs are smart. I told you we'd coddle them, and when the time came they'd work us over. They just smile and remind us of Article 9 of the 1947 Constitution which says they have to renounce war and that land, sea, and air forces are forbidden. They smile virtuously and stick to their promise. Why shouldn't they? It's not only morally correct, but much cheaper. We fork out the cash for the defence of poor little Japan – the third largest industrial power – and they put their money in the bank. In fact they bank one-third of their two hundred billion dollar gross national product – the highest rate in the world.'

'They're certainly doing well. I couldn't believe my eyes when I arrived back here. Quite a change from the occupation days when they didn't have enough rice to eat, much less a TV set. Now they have such a surplus they're storing it in disused mine shafts!'

'That was probably the start of it all. Our wealth and technical superiority caught them by surprise. They had no idea of our riches, and vowed never to be poor again. So they set out to learn from us, determined to beat us at our own game. It looks as if they've succeeded.' He opened a page of the *New York Herald Tribune*, and tossed it on to Joe's lap. The headlines spoke for themselves:

JAPAN BREAKS RECORD FOR PAYMENTS SURPLUS
JAPAN'S BILLION DOLLAR IRON CONTRACT
NEW YORK STOCK PRICES FALL TO A SIX-YEAR LOW
US OUTLOOK: THE WORST IS TO COME
JAPAN PLACES 1ST SATELLITE IN EARTH ORBIT
US MAY BECOME SECOND-CLASS POWER
TOKYO STOCK MARKET SOARS
TOKYO SHIPS: TWO YEAR BACKLOG OF ORDERS
US INFLUENCE DEFINITELY ON THE WANE

'The shoe's now on the other foot,' Garvan said, gulping his drink. 'It's the US who's harbouring a grudge.'

'But how did they manage it? So soon, I mean?'

'Good luck. And because Japan's rich in the resources that count most – the right kind of people. She lost the war, was destroyed, and so had to build her industry from scratch. A modern industry. The Korean War was a blessing in disguise, bringing in new wealth. And where once she spread her tentacles to conquer Pacific Asia, the penitent trader returned and made new friends. She's accomplished more economically than she could have done had she defeated her enemies. Australia alone supplies more raw materials than she could have expected from a puppet China.'

163

'And the right kind of people?'

'Honest, kind, hard-working, self-respecting, clean. They like mechanical things, engines and cars. They like to find out how things work. They're curious. They don't boast or belly-ache. They put success first. What succeeds is good, what fails is not for them. They're trying democracy – giving it a chance. It was victorious, so it must be good. If they find it isn't they'll drop it like a hot brick.

'They're learning our language, our way of life, our customs. They listen to us because they like us and because we've been generous and kind to them, something they didn't expect. They have no racial problems, no recession, no turmoil outside of student demonstrations, and strikes are almost unknown. It's a happy country – a busy country of a hundred million people, disciplined, well educated. I don't begrudge them their success. They're entitled to an important place in the world. On the other hand . . . ' He drained his glass and sank deeper into his chair. 'What's happening to the good old USA?'

'How do you mean?'

'We're frightened, tired, in retreat. We have a crisis of self-confidence and cross-purposes on our hands. The symptoms of defeatism and withdrawal are rife. We're giving up Okinawa because the New Left's demonstrations embarrass us, and we don't like to be disliked or unloved. And yet nobody protests about the Sakhalin Islands which the Russians pinched and have no intention of returning. The Russians don't care if they're loved or not, only for their rich rewards, while we have to pay the price for our decency. Or is it cowardice? Shame? Conceit? Vanity? The milk of human kindness? Or is it because our leaders have lost control, lost faith in their ability to control – as they have with our permissive, chaotic society, so that a sort of death wish has settled over us all from top to bottom? If this is so, my friend, it's a terrifying future we have to look forward to, you and I.'

Joe took a gulp of his own drink, feeling as if the bottom had fallen out of his stomach. He had been depressed enough these last few days!

He looked across at Garvan, who had thrown the newspaper

164

on to the floor and was lighting a cigarette, and thought to himself: You're lucky, Dennis, with the physical equipment you have, lucky to be big and quiet and steady, and with this control you have over yourself, over your body and your voice. I envy you your calm, your frank ways. You're about the frankest person I've ever met. You don't have a real laugh, not an honest-to-God laugh. You have a politeness in which a smile is involved. You're smart and you find other people a little stupid. You can be merciless and yet you can be compassionate, and you have perception, a very acute perception. You get close enough to other people, but nobody is going to get close to you. Right?

'Dennis,' he said, 'it's all very well to praise the Japanese – God knows I've been one of their most ardent admirers. Didn't I marry Hanako? But now that Naoko is getting married to one – well, I've second thoughts. Frankly I'm worried stiff. About modern Japan, I mean. This boy is an anarchist, a member of the *Zengakuren*. Everything you and I have come to love about Japan, its peace, its culture, its discipline, he wants to destroy. What am I going to do? They intend to marry in two weeks! How can I prevent it?'

'You can't. Any more than the colonels could stop you from marrying Hanako. You've got to accept it – there's nothing else you can do.'

'I can shoot him!'

'And be hanged by the neck as they hanged Hanako's brother-in-law? No, I wouldn't recommend that.'

Joe sat staring gloomily down at his drink. Garvan said: 'Don't worry about the boy, Joe. He's a student – Left Wing, yes, but there are a million and a half university students in Japan and only a few thousand end up as Communists. He wants freedom, not necessarily political freedom, but freedom from the life employment system which puts him into an airtight chamber and allows him no chance to breathe. The student revolution will spend itself as do all revolutions. Mark my word, your boy will soon settle down and become a pillar of the very society he thinks he wants to destroy.'

Joe glanced up, saw that Garvan looked suddenly tired and drawn, and said: 'It's late, Dennis. I'm sure you've had a hectic day, and I must get back myself. There's just one question. What are you going to do? Where are you going to live? Where are your roots now?'

Something very sad stole into Garvan's eyes, and Joe watched it.

'I've decided to compromise,' he said slowly. 'I've decided to stay here. My wife's coming over when my time's up at UP – when I've found a new job.'

'One last question, Dennis. Do you like the Japanese?'

'I didn't,' he said after a pause. 'And then I did.' He regarded Joe for a minute, and the old smile returned. 'Now I don't much care one way or another.'

He woke sometime during the night in a cold sweat, hearing Hanako's voice crying out to him as she stood on the airfield, the giant Army Transport plane looming behind her. She was waiting to leave for America, and he was trying to reach her before the plane took off, but he couldn't. The jeep wouldn't move. She cried out to him to hurry, her hands outstretched, and then suddenly the jeep shot forward and he was in her arms, his face buried in her hair.

For a long time he lay in the darkness, thinking about her, about his talk with Dennis Garvan, about his trip to Japan, and slowly everything became clear to him. After the wedding he would go home, not necessarily to London, or America, or Europe, but to Hanako. Home. That at least was a single good service Mrs Jane Conway Ogihara had done for him, quite unwittingly. All these years he had tied their love to a dream of a forgotten land. He had wanted roots, a home, security, when all the time she was his security. He had been too blind to recognize the fact.

They had their differences, their adversities, but what married couple didn't? They were no longer young honeymooners, but mature people living in an immature society. They were two fragile human beings in a world gone mad, and they needed each other. They needed each other to give them courage to endure it, to live in it, to live with themselves. Whatever the cause of their past difficulties, they would have to be faced and

166

overcome, because without each other there was no hope and no purpose. Home was wherever people loved. If he and Hanako were one, as they were, why seek or question that One? It was as simple as that.

He had found disenchantment and disappointment around every corner, but it was not because of any desperation on his part that he was returning to Hanako; on the contrary, in this new Japan he had found her again, an Hanako cleansed and transfigured against the backdrop of a world now alien to them both, a world that did not need their admiration or their pity, a world that had passed them by.

So be it. They had each other. Thank God they had each other! He would send her a telegram in the morning telling her of his decision.

Naoko crept into the room and kissed him good night. Her hair, scented with gardenia, brought back visions of the Japan he once knew and loved, and when she had gone, closing the door softly behind her, he lay in a state of half-dream remembering the people he had met, the places he had visited, the odd things he had seen and done, alone or with strangers he had mingled with: the blind masseuses whose outstretched arms reached out to him from a dark alley, the deaf shoeshine women, the beggars with their rented children. The members of the *chin-don-ya* tribes, the ragpickers, the beauties of the geisha guild. The lunchtime golfers and volley-ball players, the sweet singing choristers of the noontime break. The kids in mountain-climbing rig, the kids with their cameras, the kids in their identical uniforms. The squatting throwbacks in topknots and belly bands. The slim, sloe-eyed girls in the doors of the coffee shops. The maniacs crouched behind the wheels. The quiet folk in the shrines and temples, anointing their faces with sacred water.

Scenes returned to him in a sort of endless montage: the Kurakuza roller-coaster, the Sumida River coal barges, the movie crowds letting out at Yurakuza, the bookstalls and snake-file remedies of Kanda, the rush-hour frenzy of Marunouchi and Otemachi. A ballerina's fluffed skirt, a dusk sky fiery with the setting sun, a young couple testing hi-fi at Akihabara, a taste of hormones grilled on a spit over charcoal, a ship sliding down the ways, a fireworks festival, a dolls' festival . . .

Tokyo was a sanctuary, he dreamily thought. It was also a trap, a treasure house of hope and despair. One could hate it, one could love it. One could never forget it.

Chapter Twenty-one

The service was held on the top floor of the Mitsukoshi department store in Nihonbashi. It seemed to Joe a strange place to hold a wedding, especially for a militant member of the *Zengakuren*, as the store was the epitome of big business. It took in over two million dollars every Sunday, as no doubt it would do again today while the wedding was in progress. However, the room was a modern, up-to-date replica of an ancient Shinto shrine, and though it lacked the mystery of the woodland and the scent of the pines, the service was no different from the one Joe had experienced at his wedding to Hanako nineteen years before.

A double line of chairs ran down each side of the room, one section reserved for the groom's relatives and friends, the other for the bride's family. Joe was escorted by an usher to his section and was surprised to find Morimoto already seated in the first row, dressed in his elegant dark kimono and *hakama* stamped with his crest. He knew that Naoko had written to him, but he never dreamed the old man would come all this way on the train by himself to be present at her wedding. They bowed to one another, but Morimoto did not speak, and then both turned their attention to the altar where the priest in his white kimono and winged sleeves was preparing the *sake* and arranging the cushions on the floor for the bridal couple.

Across the room the groom's parents and friends were already seated – Takashi Sumitomo looking very prosperous and severe in striped trousers and morning coat, Mrs Sumitomo in a pale blue ceremonial kimono. In the second row a scatter-ing of Naruhito's student friends lounged about in various stages of undress.

Joe waited impatiently for Naoko and the boy to appear. He had not seen her bridal gown which she had rented, and was flabbergasted when she finally appeared by the side of her young man, almost unrecognizable in black tie, high stiff collar, and morning suit.

Joe knew that Naoko had been unable to decide until the last minute whether to wear a Western bridal gown and veil, or a kimono, and he was taken aback, not only by the splendour of her costume, but by the realization that he had really lost her now, lost her for ever to this boy, a total stranger, and to this far Eastern land to which he would never return.

Seeing her on her knees, her head bowed in prayer beneath the priest's feather wand, her costume alone seemed to set her forever apart from him and from all that he had associated her with: her English school, her little room in the mews, her own mother. She was dressed in a snow-white silk kimono em-broidered with three designs of delicate colours with a two-foot brocaded *obi* tied in an intricate bow at the back. Her wig was made up into a stunning *shimada* coiffure bedecked with hair-pins and decorated with plum blossoms, tortoise shells and coral. On top of this was placed the *tsunokakushi*, the triangular band to cover the horns of jealousy which all women possessed. He sat stunned, close to tears, as the priest addressed the deity, chanting his offering for the couple's protection and future happiness.

As Joe listened to the voice drone on and on, he was lifted, as if by a wave, and transported to a place of beauty, strange to him, and yet familiar, in that it was not only a temple, a lake, a park, a mountain, but all of these, a place of silence filled with kaleidoscopic tints, the fleeting reflection of willows in water, the fluid snow of cherry blossoms.

The shadow of evening fell over the sacred ground. Only a few stone lanterns glimmered in the twilight. The wind had subsided. Silence descended upon the motionless trees – a silence of life appeased.

By listening intently he could catch the murmur of things: a grouse in her pine-tree roost, the bark of a weasel, the brittle click of a cicada, the whimper of a bear cub, the rustle of a deer mouse. All was peace, tolerance, serenity.

Suddenly there was a blinding flash of vision, a lightning flash that held for several seconds. He was not dreaming. His lucid thought was seeking in good faith to understand himself, other men, other consciences, other reasons. He understood at once, completely and beyond all argument, the whole problem of self and selfishness, of suffering and the cause of suffering. The ability to understand, to grasp life's endless pluralities and entanglements, did not come from without, but from within. Little by little, unknown mystical values awakened in him as the impurities of his body and mind fell away, fell to the bottom of the alley, lost in the swirling mist.

Like a fool he tried to explain his vision, and it fled.

He walked away, detached from himself, detached even from his own detachment. He went, indifferent as the breeze that had mysteriously sprung up, towards the East and the West, like a leaf detached from its branch.

He came upon a little shrine, a simple wooden hut containing a basin of lustral water. Bending down, he saw that the clear surface reflected his face – and then, surprisingly, two faces, the other the face of a lovely dark-haired girl who smiled back at him. He had seen the face before somewhere, he was sure of it. But it had not been a happy face, as this face was. It had been full of pain and unhappiness, a troubled, frightened face. Obviously the pure fresh water had washed the unhappiness away. He had never believed until now that one could free one's self of all worry and discontent merely by crossing the threshold of a rustic shrine, but seeing her radiant expression, he knew it was true. This simple wooden hut lived upon a secret. Here one forgot. Here one created one's self anew.

But now her face had vanished. He looked up and saw that the girl was watching him. He wondered at her puzzled glance. It seemed that he remembered her voice: 'I kiss your hands which are so white. I kiss your feet that they may bring you to me without delay. Oh, *anata*, I love you so much!'

170

Then why did she run away? She was running through the wood as if carried by the wind. Or was it she who carried the wind? And there were tears in her eyes. But this could not be, for Hanako never cried. Were they, then, his own tears?

'Joe-san . . . '

Her voice hammered at his brain. He closed his eyes in an effort to shut it out. Oh, God, why was she running away!

'Joe, please listen to me! Are you not well? You disturb honourable ceremony. People wonder what is the matter with you!'

He took his hands from his eyes, and stared at her. She couldn't be real! Hanako sitting beside him? Hanako in a kimono! Hanako in Japan! It was impossible. And yet . . .

He was distracted by Morimoto seated at her side. He had turned and was studying her with a vague, blank, frigid expression. Did he recognize his daughter-in-law? Would he speak to her? Insult her, cause a commotion, stomp from the room?

Hanako, following his gaze, became aware of the old man's presence for the first time. She stiffened, and bowed. Morimoto's expression remained frozen, immobile, and then after what seemed an eternity, he acknowledged her greeting with an almost imperceptible nod of his head, accompanied by a flicker of a smile.

Now Joe had eyes only for Hanako. It was the first time he had seen her in her national dress for years. She seemed taller, more buxom, more beautiful, poised, relaxed, her eyes shining as of old, yet with a strange new light as she reached for his hand and guided it beneath the folds of her kimono, so that he felt there the reason for her buxomness, felt his unborn child alive and moving within her.

Now the bride and groom were sipping from the little lacquer wine-cups. Three times they sipped the *sake*, drinking alternately until all the wine had been consumed, signifying that husband and wife were partners for joy and for sorrow, for better or for worse. And then the husband picked up his cup and crossed the room to offer the wine to his parents, and likewise the wife went to offer her cup to her father. Her astonishment, her delight at finding her mother seated beside him, their fingers clasped tightly together, was equalled only by the happiness in her heart when Naruhito joined her, took her arm, and ushered her into the reception room where the guests were waiting.

If you have enjoyed this
PAN Book you may like
to choose your next book
from the titles listed on the
following pages.

Pearl S. Buck

Peter O'Donnell

Modesty Blaise and her henchman Willie
Garvin – a duo of heroic dimensions – come
across everything: violence, sex, torture,
man-to-man combat, spy-stuff, medicine . . .
Great fun!

I LUCIFER   35p

'In the past forty-eight hours a poison capsule
had been cut out of her body . . . she had fought
a carefully faked duel; made a four-hour swim,
paddled a canoe for six hours, slept for ten,
tested her shoulder in combat, made complex
plans and preparations. And now . . .'

THE IMPOSSIBLE VIRGIN   30p

On a fast and furious caper to Central Africa,
Modesty and Willie land in the tightest spots –
facing professional killers, maddened gorillas,
savage warriors and the ferocious guardians of
The Impossible Virgin . . .

Leslie Thomas

'A marvellously inventive and endearing writer with an undoubted gift for writing up comic and tender moments in and around bed' – THE OBSERVER

THE VIRGIN SOLDIERS   30p

The virgin soldiers did not ask to be conscripted; they did not ask to fight. On the brink of war they all wanted to make one frantic attempt at living before dying . . .
'Truthfully, tough, wildly sexy, hilariously funny, and as modern as tomorrow' – Carl Foreman

THE LOVE BEACH   35p

Preparations for a Royal visit to their fabled South Sea island – a twilight colony ridden with petty jealousies, social taboos and love affairs – bring problems for everyone . . .

COME TO THE WAR   30p

Non-stop action amid the blankets and bullets of the not-so-virgin soldiers of Israel during the Six Day War . . .

These and other PAN Books are obtainable from all booksellers and newsagents. If you have any difficulty please send purchase price plus 7p postage to PO Box 11, Falmouth, Cornwall.
While every effort is made to keep prices low, it is sometimes necessary to increase prices at short notice. PAN Books reserve the right to show new retail prices on covers which may differ from those advertised in the text or elsewhere.